"Dance with m[...] into Charlie's bar and onto the floor, pulling her tight against him.

Jackie rested her head against his shoulder as they caught the slow beat.

It seemed to Gray he'd been waiting for hours to get her into his arms. Her hair smelled of spring flowers, and there was a trace of some deeper scent, like perfumed soap, under that. His arms tightened around her, and she felt a burning from her chest to her thighs, at the tips of her fingers and palms. Everywhere they touched.

A gasp escaped her lips when he pulled her hips tight against him. For a second she saw herself on his bed, with him lying over her as he had the night she'd brought him home. She tried to draw back, but Gray wouldn't let her.

"Stay." His breath tickled her ear. He rubbed his rough cheek against hers and moved her from side to side, whirled her around until her head fell back. Then the song ended and the band went into another one she remembered from long ago.

Gray's bright, clear eyes looked into hers with open heat. She traced the creases that fanned out from them and one tiny mark from the chicken pox near his left brow. His warm hands slid over her back from her waist to her shoulders, up and down as if he couldn't stop.

When the song was over, he drew her hand to his mouth and kissed the inside of her wrist.

The guy made her breath catch. No kidding.

Then he took her out of there. They never even had a table. . . .

WHAT ARE *LOVESWEPT* ROMANCES?

They are stories of true romance and touching emotion. We believe those two very important ingredients are constants in our highly sensual and very believable stories in the *LOVESWEPT* line. Our goal is to give you, the reader, stories of consistently high quality that may sometimes make you laugh, sometimes make you cry, but are always fresh and creative and contain many delightful surprises within their pages.

Most romance fans read an enormous number of books. Those they truly love, they keep. Others may be traded with friends and soon forgotten. We hope that each *LOVESWEPT* romance will be a treasure—a "keeper." We will always try to publish

LOVE STORIES YOU'LL NEVER FORGET
BY AUTHORS YOU'LL ALWAYS REMEMBER

The Editors

Kimberli Wagner
A Cowboy's Touch

BANTAM BOOKS
NEW YORK · TORONTO · LONDON · SYDNEY · AUCKLAND

A COWBOY'S TOUCH

A Bantam Book / September 1992

If you would be interested in receiving protective vinyl
covers for your Loveswept books, please write to this address
for information:

> *Loveswept*
> *Bantam Books*
> *P.O. Box 985*
> *Hicksville, NY 11802*

ISBN 0-553-44283-X

Published simultaneously in the United States and Canada

PRINTED IN THE UNITED STATES OF AMERICA

OPM   0 9 8 7 6 5 4 3 2 1

One

Jackie gave a start as Hank slammed a full glass on her tray and glared over her shoulder. Following Hank's gaze, she stole a glance back at the cowboy who sat alone, stacking shot glasses next to longneck bottles.

A knot of emotion tightened her throat, and she set her jaw. After all, she'd known it had to happen sometime. Sooner or later, she'd run into him in a town this size.

His hat was tipped back as far as it could go without falling off. Swaying in his chair, he pushed it into place again. Once the brim was settled firmly over his eyes, he grunted and raised an empty bottle to order another drink.

Gray Burton, Jackie thought. Ex-bull-riding champion . . . town celebrity.

She sighed and a tremor shook her hand. Even now he still had that same effect on her. *Why?* She squeezed her eyes shut and gave a frustrated snort.

He looked the same; long and lean with power-ful thighs. The strong nose and angled jaw were as familiar as her own, but his skin was dark from years of sun, his expression more harsh than she remembered.

He still had a beautiful mouth.

"Perfect," she muttered as she watched him trying to keep his head from falling to his chest.

He'd come in hours ago with five friends: two women, three men. They sat crowded around a table, Gray's arm encircling a perky blonde with too much makeup.

Walking to that table was one of the hardest things she'd ever had to do. And she'd known Hank was taking special pleasure in seeing Gray Burton watch his ex-wife wait tables in Hank's bar. But she needed the job, so she had made that long walk.

Gray had looked up, and she'd seen every expression melt from his face. His arm had started to fall from the shoulders of the blonde, until he realized what he was doing and snagged the girl closer in defiance.

Silence fell around them as he'd stared at Jackie.

"Well," he'd drawled at last, his hand moving to play with a strand of the blonde's hair, "look who's come to town."

Then he'd ordered a beer and a shot as if they'd never met before, as if they'd never . . . anything.

Flushing deeply, Jackie had turned on her heel and gotten their drinks.

She didn't know his friends, and he soon waved them off to greener pastures, even the squeezable blonde. Then he sat alone, drinking shots of te-quila as he brooded and watched her wait tables.

Now, it was ten minutes to closing and the place had started to clear out. The jukebox was playing Willie Nelson, and was too loud without people there. She'd never seen Gray drink more than a couple of beers before, and it made her uneasy that he'd drunk so much. But it really wasn't any of her business.

She put the beer he'd ordered down and watched his brows pull together in concentration as he dragged a wad of bills from a tight front pocket.

"Is somebody at the house who'd come to get you, Graham?" she finally asked, thinking how strange his name sounded to her ears.

"Nope." Gray leaned forward and took stock of her, from ankles, over tight jeans, and up to a frilly Mexican blouse. His gaze lingered there. The look of her was so damn familiar, even after seven long years. Lush, soft. Her eyes tilted like a cat's, and her pale hair flowed in waves over bare shoulders. He thought her curves were a little fuller than they'd been seven years ago. His hands itched to circle her waist to see.

How she'd haunted him. How she'd torn him into little pieces. Even now, the sight of her brought it all back, every torturous memory. But he couldn't make himself leave, and he couldn't stop looking.

Her soft mouth was pursed in disapproval. He thought that was funny, funny as hell. She was disapproving of *him* getting drunk because it was so damn hard to see her again. What about what she had done?

"Don' wan' to go home," he said, tilting his head back and grinning at her. "I wanna talk . . . about why you're here."

She frowned down at him. "That's none of your business."

"You stayin'?" he asked, trying to sound casual.

"How about if I give you a call when I decide?" She turned and started to walk away.

He pushed his hat back with one finger. "You still got the purtiest hair I ever saw, Jack," he said, his Texas accent strong and pure.

Jackie's steps faltered. Then she remembered he was drunk. She wondered how he was going to feel when he tried to stand up.

"Hey!" he went on. "You wanna gimme a ride home?"

She glanced back at him. "I don't think so."

He pursed his lips and shrugged. "Okay. Maybe you c'n call me a taxi. Still got dough. I c'n pay what it takes." He waved a hundred dollar bill in the air, and she saw another in his left hand. "Gotta get home."

She raised a brow and said in a tight voice, "Yeah, you still got dough. I'll call you a cab." *Well, what did you expect?* she asked herself as she watched him shrug away her rejection.

"He can't drive, Hank," she said to the bar owner. "You want to call a cab?"

Gray was humming along to the music as the big, barrel-chested man came out from behind the bar.

"Ain't my problem and it ain't yours," Hank announced, a gleam in his eye. "But he's goin' out . . . ooh-yeh-siree. You collect for that last drink?" Hank's round belly hung over his belt, and he rubbed at a wet spot on his shirt.

"Got change for a hundred?" she asked him. There was a strange look on his beefy face. She'd always known there was some bad feeling between him and Gray, but neither had ever said why. She didn't like Hank's look, though.

Gray's eyes had closed, so she tugged the money from his hand.

Hank's lips turned up in a slick smile. "As a matter of fact"—he grabbed the bill from her and stuffed it into his shirt pocket, then snatched the other from Gray's lax fingers—"I do."

"Give it back, Hank," Jackie said.

"Give what back?" He turned a hard look her way.

Her own expression was just as stiff. "Give him his money."

"I don't know what you're talking about, little britches. But I think it's time for you to cash out and go on home. This good ole boy and me are gonna have a conversation before he gets some fresh air." The look he gave Gray was full of menace.

"What? Am I supposed to just let you do anything you want to him?" Jackie held on to her brown plastic tray like a weapon. "Give him the money back, Hank."

"Says who?" Hank scowled down at her. "You think I take orders from any cute piece of tail who can wag it and carry a beer five feet?" He took her arm and gripped it so tightly, she winced and tried to twist away. "Your name ain't Burton anymore!"

She glared at him. "Let go."

Hank didn't release her. Instead he tightened his fingers as she tried to squirm out of his grasp. "I didn't have to give you this job," he said. "And I can replace what you think you got in thirty seconds. So just keep outta this!"

"Let go!" She tugged at his hand with her free one, trying to remember the self-defense moves she had learned the year before. "You're hurting me!"

Gray might have been a bit confused by all the conversation going on, but when he heard Jack say that, he staggered up out of sheer reflex. He was surprised he wasn't quite steady.

"Hey, big man," he said.

Hank smiled. It wasn't a nice smile. He released Jackie and dusted off his hands.

"You want a piece of me, Burton?" he asked, and on the last word, he hit Gray a glancing blow off one cheek. Gray fell back a step before he recovered, then his right fist slammed into Hank's face. Hank went down like a stone.

"Ohhhmygod," Jackie breathed, and her tray fell to the floor with a whack and a clatter. Leaning over Hank's body, she stared. "Now you've done it! You don't think he's dead, do you?" Finally, she saw the barrel chest rise and fall. She looked up as Gray was reaching blindly for his chair.

"Oh, no, you don't." She grabbed his waving arm with both hands and hauled him away. "We've got to get out of here, as fast and as far as we can." Pulling Gray to the bar, she leaned him there while she got her purse. Then she put one arm around his hard waist and guided him to the door. "Wait a minute." She stopped. "You stay right here." She pushed him against the doorjamb and went back for his money.

Her fingers were an inch away from Hank's shirt pocket, when he groaned and moved his head. She gasped and jerked her hand back, deciding her broken bones were worth more than two hundred dollars that Gray Burton wouldn't even miss.

So she ran back to Gray, grabbed his belt, and towed him out the door.

Only one car was out front, Jackie's ancient pink Rambler. Her heart was beating in her temples, and her hands trembled as she got Gray into the front seat and shut the door. As she hurried

around to the driver's side, she saw Hank stagger
outside with a crowbar.

Nobody on the street, no cars . . .

"Start, Baby," she prayed, slamming her door
shut. "Please start." She turned the key, flipped
open the glove compartment, and squeezed the
red and gray wires there. The car turned over, and
Jackie peeled out of the gravel drive, chanting,
"Thank you thank you thank you . . ."

A glance in the rearview mirror showed Hank
waving the crowbar, his mouth moving fast. She
let out the breath she'd been holding too long and
sat back in the seat.

Then she heard it.

She turned in amazement to the man leaning
against the passenger door. Hat tipped over his
face, arms crossed and legs spread wide, he was
snoring!

Jackie's hands tightened on the wheel as she
ground her teeth. Then she looked straight ahead,
aiming for a great, big, black pothole!

By the time Jackie pulled into the long drive
that led to the Burton property, she'd been mut-
tering to herself for ten minutes. In all the crazi-
ness, she'd left her tip cup on the bar. Damn! The
gas gauge had been on empty for the last two
miles, and she didn't have any money with her. All
because she had tried to keep her rich ex-
husband from being rolled. As if he would even
know the difference!

The stables were lit by floodlights, but they were
some distance from the house. Only a porch light
shone from the sprawling two-story structure.

Now what? she wondered, as she braked to a
stop and turned to look at the man next to her.

The stubble on his jaw had a reddish glint, and his beautiful, sculpted lips were relaxed. His neck was bent at an uncomfortable angle.

She almost tipped his hat back for a better look, when he made a rusty-sounding noise. She jumped back to stare solemnly at the windshield. After a moment, she bit her lip and turned, oh so slowly, to find his eyes closed. After staring for a full minute, she finally sighed.

"Jacqueline Stone, you are a donkey's behind," she told herself. She cranked her door open and stalked around to his side. Impatient just to have this night over, she threw open his door, only to have to catch him as all six feet two inches of him spilled out, headfirst.

"Wake up, Junior! I am not dragging your carcass into that house by the hair . . . " She was still talking to him as she finally stuffed him upright in the seat and mashed his hat squarely upon his head. "You're too damned big!"

His eyes still closed, he looked confused, as if there were something he could figure out if he just tried very, very hard. Then the blue eyes opened, and he smiled at her for two seconds before his eyes closed again.

Jackie couldn't believe it! He was getting to her, drunk and half out of it, he was still getting to her. She steeled herself, willing stiffness into her spine, willing herself to remember what this cowboy was like, with his easy charm, quick temper, and selfish ways.

"Wake up!" She stamped her foot for emphasis. "Now!"

Nothing.

She stood for a moment, then nudged his leg with her foot. It just wagged back to where it had been before.

"All right, then. I don't really know what a happy drunk is, but I hope you're it." She took a deep breath, raised her right hand, and slapped his cheek.

His fist came from nowhere—his eyes weren't even open. And she was lucky that she was almost out of range, because even at that distance he laid her flat on the ground.

She lay there, shocked, one hand to her jaw, trying hard to get her bearings.

He hit me! she thought, fury clouding her vision. Puffing hard, she was cussing like a dry-docked sailor when she scrambled to her feet and lunged at him. Grabbing the front of his shirt with both hands, she yanked all hundred and ninety pounds from her car and glared into his face.

He blinked like a dear, puzzled owl.

Her fury drained away as quickly as it had come. "Uhm, Graham?" she tried, holding him up by his shirt. "Junior? Uh, you think you can walk?" She steadied him, thoroughly embarrassed by the way her pulse raced just from touching him.

Gray shook his head to clear it, but her words meant nothing to him. He couldn't even see straight.

"You want to sit down a minute?" he heard someone say.

"I'm home?" he asked, recognizing the outline of the main house.

"Yes," the voice answered.

"Good."

Slowly, he straightened and took a step forward, then he was striding along with Jackie trotting close behind. She followed him as he circled the house, passed the pool, and made his unsteady way to a smaller structure. It hadn't been there when they were married. Not that she'd stayed long at the Burton ranch.

Gray stamped up onto the porch and braced himself against the front door.

"You open it," he mumbled.

She had to step under one of his outstretched arms to reach it. Hitching that arm over her shoulders, she helped him stand again. He smelled of beer and man, leather and sweat, and she closed her eyes to block out the memories. The muscles of his arm flexed against her neck. She firmed her mouth and walked him inside.

Curious, she glanced around. It wasn't a mansion. The decor was comfortable—though expensive comfortable—warm beiges and cream. Ahead was a curving staircase with a rosewood banister and thick cranberry carpeting.

"Where?" she asked him, and he looked toward the top of the stairs and gave a kind of grunt.

She sighed. "Okay. Let's go."

By the time they reached the top, she was pushing from behind, her hands on his hips. How could she have forgotten how big he was?

On the second floor landing, he grunted again and hooked an arm around her. Grinning a dopey grin, he dragged her forward so he could lean more heavily, then they moved down the hall.

Finally, he pushed open the last door. The room was dark, but Gray walked ahead with a sure instinct for the bed as the hall light streamed in behind them.

Jackie glanced around the dark room as he sat on the edge of the mattress.

"Boots," he muttered as he knocked his curly-brimmed hat off with one hand. It rolled across the floor. Jackie put her hands on her hips at his tone, and he looked up with a provoking grin. "What you waitin' on, darlin'?"

"Not a thing, *darlin'*," she answered in a splintery voice. Did he have any idea which "darlin'" he was talking to, she wondered, and wished this would be over before her headache got any worse. Then she thought that as long as she was wishing, she'd wish she didn't want things she couldn't have.

He squinted up at her, and his words were slurred. "Jack, tha's you, ain't it?"

That froze her in her tracks, until he spoke again.

"Need help with ma boots, sweet'eart." His white teeth gleamed in the half-light.

"Yeah," she said, and sighed as she swung a leg over his to assume the position. Her jaw was aching, and she felt a little dizzy at this angle. All she wanted was to lie down in the wide backseat of her car and get a few hours sleep.

Tomorrow, she would worry about gas money and another job and getting her pay from Hank. She'd have to wait a bit longer to decide everything that had to be decided. She did have some emergency cash in the teapot over the stove at her dad's place.

Jackie supposed Gray thought she wasn't getting that boot off fast enough, because he tried to help by pushing his other big foot against the back pocket of her jeans. When she straightened in surprise, the right boot slid off in her hands. It fell through her fingers and hit the floor with a loud thump.

Slapping at the back of her jeans, she said, "I can do it just fine!" Then she grabbed the boot he still wore and almost pulled him from the bed trying to get it off.

As soon as it came away, Gray quit playing possum. He snaked an arm around her waist and tugged.

Surprise whistled through her lips as her world tilted. She found herself lying face up on his bed, the heel of his left boot still clutched in both hands.

A choking sound came from deep in her throat as Gray braced an elbow on either side of her body and leaned his chest upon her torso. One strong thigh was wedged between hers. His eyes were half-closed, and his smile seemed to slam into her belly.

"Mmmm," he whispered, and lowered his head.

Heat rushed through her, then panic, as his lips touched hers. His mouth was so hot, so coaxingly sweet. He tasted of tequila and man and . . . Junior Burton.

When he groaned aloud, she twisted, shoving his hard boot into his chest and pushing to get free.

But he changed the kiss as his hand found her breast, and she was stunned to stillness. Her heartbeat hammered in her ears, and her breath shortened. Sensation rushed from her breast and settled between her thighs in a bolt of raw lightning.

No . . . she cried silently.

"Baby," he whispered. "Ah, baby, you feel so good." He sighed. "You like that . . . I know you, sweetheart. I know you do." His voice caressed her, and she shuddered in response. Gray looked down at her, rubbing lightly around and over the crest of her breast as he somehow maneuvered the boot from between them. He pushed his thigh higher, pressing against the embarrassing heat between her legs. "Ah, Jack."

Jackie swallowed hard and stared into those eyes that so weakened her, had always weakened her.

"Oh . . . don't," she said, and spoiled it with a sigh. "No," she tried again, though her voice was still weak.

He only grinned and slid down far enough to kiss a chill-raising trail from her chin to her collarbone. Her eyes drifted shut.

Nothing ever . . . ever felt like this.

Her skin seemed to be shimmering, and beneath it, her heart pounded in starts and stutters.

Forcing her eyes open, she pulled air into her lungs, struggling for calm, only to cry out when his mouth closed over her breast.

"Junior," she gasped.

His lips kissed all around her breast with a slow, erotic intensity. Finally, he took the tight center into his mouth, biting through crisp cotton. Jackie's hips jerked up in reflex. He groaned again, rubbing his lips and teeth over her as if he couldn't have enough.

She should have been outraged, screaming or something. He didn't even really know it was she, she thought, squeezing her eyes shut. Still, she didn't stop it. *Why wasn't she stopping it?*

"So sweet," he breathed, melting her. Then he laid his cheek upon her breast, letting his weight fall to the side of her, and began to snore.

Again.

She tensed, certain that the sound had to be something else. But he moved his head, settling more comfortably into her shoulder, breathing deeply.

Furious at both of them, Jackie humphed and tried to throw him off her. He wouldn't budge. She stared at the ceiling, talking herself into calming down. Finally, she wiggled out from under him. He tugged her back as if she were a favorite teddy bear and rubbed his beard-roughened cheek against hers.

It's okay, she told herself as she laughed. He always had slept like the dead. she'd just wait until his muscles relaxed, then she'd slip out.

Crazy.

Two

Curled up in the backseat of her Rambler, fifteen minutes later, Jackie rubbed her cheeks hard with both hands. How would she face Gray in the morning? Would he even remember what had happened?

She pulled the scratchy blanket she'd found in the trunk up to her sore chin and squirmed again, her gaze fixed on the worn cloth ceiling of the car.

Junior.

She hadn't even known how lonely she'd been until he touched her. She'd never acted like that in her life . . . except with him. A shiver of memory dashed down her spine, of how he'd felt beside her at night, and of other ways he'd felt.

She thought of Graham at eighteen. He'd been years older than she, with his pick of rich debs with white convertibles and long, tanned legs. The Burton ranch had been one of the biggest in the county, so Graham, Jr. had been considered quite the catch before he even made it past junior high.

Every Sunday, there he'd be, standing straight and tall in the Burton pew with his father and mother, and his brothers, Tom and Ben. The boys' shirts were always white and starch-stiff. Most times the older boys kept their eyes forward, but there were still moments when they looked around for diversion from a dull sermon.

Jackie would drink her fill of his profile then, as he glanced past her and on to doe-eyed Becky Timms or boy-crazy Sarah Jane Norman. Lord knew they were eager enough to try to fix his interest, smirking and fidgeting, Becky even fanning herself with the hymn program like she felt faint.

Jackie had figured he'd never even seen her, the skinny kid with ragged yellow pigtails and big eyes, who sent longing glances his way so many Sundays.

Finally, he did see her.

He had been her storybook hero come to life and the one person in the world who understood her. Her whole life had centered on what would please him.

But that was a long time ago. A very long time ago.

She fell asleep with the feel of his lips on her mouth, her skin, and a heavy aching in her heart.

The next thing Jackie knew, a plump, middle-aged woman with copper hair, freckles, and a cherub's face was leaning in the car window at her feet.

"Ah, don't know," the cherub drawled in an east Texas twang. "If Ah'd spent a night like that, Ah'd want a cup of my coffee real bad." She grinned. "Ah'm Merle."

Jackie was sitting up by that time. She pushed

her hair back, squeezed her eyes tight, and tried to focus.

"You say something about coffee?"

"Just follow me, honey," Merle said, and started back to the big house.

Jaw aching and body stiff as cardboard, Jackie fumbled for her shoes and purse. She sort of fell out of the car and followed, not even worrying about her hair going in all directions.

She walked around to the back door and entered the giant, cheery kitchen. Merle pointed to the first door down the hallway and said, "Fresh towels in there, kid."

Jackie smiled her thanks.

When she came out, face scrubbed and teeth towel brushed, Merle was cracking eggs into a skillet. "How do you like 'em?" she asked over her shoulder.

Jackie felt she had no choice but to give in gracefully. Anything else would mean discussion before coffee. "Over easy," she said, and smiled shyly.

"Coffee's on the table." Merle turned back to the eggs.

Jackie sat down at the long, worn oak table and poured herself a cup from the china pot.

When the eggs were done, Merle sat down with her own cup of coffee and passed the basket of blueberry muffins already on the table. Jackie was almost finished eating before Merle said thoughtfully, "Bill Stone's girl, aren't ya? Used to be married to Gray."

"Jackie," she introduced herself. "Did you know my dad?"

"Enough to say hello." Merle put sugar in her cup, banging the spoon noisily. She was obviously a woman who did everything with enthusiasm.

"We'd run into each other up at Frog Lake sometimes. He liked to fish, so do I. I was real sorry to hear about the accident."

Jackie's gaze moved to the window and beyond, and she kept her expression carefully blank. He'd been gone for a month, and she still found it hard to think about him. So little time ago her dad had been a vibrant, healthy man. They didn't see each other much, but no matter what their problems, she had always known he loved her.

Then she'd gotten the call from the county sheriff. Her dad had fallen from the hayloft onto a truck bed, breaking his neck.

Jackie had left her job at the university and come home. She'd talked to the police, who had found it to be an accident. When she'd gone through her father's papers, she'd discovered that he had emptied his ranch accounts, everything but his personal account. He'd even mortgaged the property.

All for one gamble on one foal.

"Bill Stone was a good man." Merle's warm voice brought her back to the bright kitchen.

"A damn good man." Jackie smiled for Merle, because she had been kind. "Here's to 'im." She touched her mug to Merle's, and they drank.

That was how Gray found them.

His hair was wet and his feet bare, and he wore a denim shirt and jeans. He looked like "the morning after the fight," and her heart started that crazy rhythm at the first sight of him at the back door.

So she was really there, Gray thought. Right there within reach.

"You're up late, ain't cha?" Merle said. "Holy moe!" She leaned way back in her chair as she got a better look at him. "That a shiner I see? The other guy look as good as you?"

Gray pushed his hand through his hair, and color stained his neck as he cleared his throat. He winced when he squinted, testing his bruised eye, then stepped forward and filled a mug with black coffee. He gave Jackie the once-over as he raised his cup, his gaze lingering on the swollen side of her jaw.

"What's *she* doing here?" he finally asked Merle.

"Now ain't that funny." Merle grinned. "Ah was sure you'd know all about it, seein' as how she's the one got you home last night."

"I can understand that you might not remember," Jackie said, staring boldly at him.

"I remember"—his gaze slid over her shirt down to the curve of her breasts and returned to her eyes—"the face."

"Thanks for breakfast, Merle," she said, pushing back her chair and standing. "It was great. But if you wouldn't mind too much, I need to talk to Graham alone for a minute."

He grimaced into his cup. He hated it when she called him Graham.

"Sure, honey, sure." Merle was already bustling into the hallway. "Last thing Ah want to do is mix in. Ah'll be upstairs."

Gray sat down in the chair Merle had vacated, his long legs sprawled out before him. He still needed a shave, Jackie saw, and the bruises around his eye and on his cheek were blue and purple.

How could she ever have thought of this stern-faced man as her gentle hero?

"I need to borrow five dollars," she aid finally.

"I thought I gave last night." One eyebrow slid up as he gave her a sidelong glance. "Though I do wish I had a better memory of what was worth two hundred dollars. Were you good to me, Jack?"

He couldn't have slapped her harder with an open hand. Jackie huffed and wished Hank had blackened his other eye too. She controlled her temper with some difficulty. "Hank took your money," she said coldly.

"Then why don't you ask Hank for your five dollars?"

It took only seconds for that to sink in, but when it did, her cheeks blazed and her accent came out.

"Why you . . . high-and-mighty . . . son of a brayin' jackass! Of course you have to draw the worst conclusions. You always did. You don't really remember a thing about last night, do you?" Her furious gaze pinned him. "You're missing a couple hundred bucks, so now I'm not just a whore, I'm a two-hundred-dollar whore—and I'm conniving with Hank Turner? For your information, *cowboy,* I wouldn't sleep with you for a hundred times that. And don't think I care if you believe what I say anymore. But just so you've got it straight this time—I lost my job and a night's tips trying to keep Hank from bashing in your fat head for that bank account you carry around in your pocket like bait!" Snagging her purse, she whirled around to the hallway, so she wouldn't have to step over his legs to get out of his blasted house!

As she strode past the stairs, she saw that the wall was still covered with photos of Gray at different events, riding broncs, riding bulls. All of them were action shots of him in spectacular, balletlike rides.

"Jerk!" she spat out under her breath.

"Hey, wait a minute," he called from behind her. That didn't even slow her down.

"Jack!"

Outside, she opened her car door and slammed it shut after her. Grinding her teeth, she flipped open the glove compartment and started the engine. She mashed her foot down on the accelerator, gunning the motor. The Rambler rumbled and shook, but it moved.

Still fuming, Jackie turned the wheel to follow the circle of the gravel drive and saw Gray standing barefoot in the dirt. Then she looked at her gas gauge and got even madder. She headed right for him, stomping on the brake at the same time he jumped out of her path.

The man always had been quick on his feet, she thought, and cursed.

She got out and yelled at him, "You *owe* me!" Her hands gripped both hips. "Five bucks. That's all I want from you. Only thing I ever asked, damn you. Five bucks for saving your pointed head from being cracked open by an iron bar! I never asked for any part of your big bucks or your precious ranch, but by God you can lend me five dollars for saving your measly behind last night." Her fury made her tremble. "Just give it to me, dammit!"

"Jack, can you calm down a minute so we can talk?" Gray thought he sounded reasonable, but Jackie wasn't in a mood to listen.

"If you don't give me five dollars this instant," she said, pointing a finger at him, "I'm gonna tell every female in this little town that you've got the biggest equipment and the worst case of premature . . . overexcitement I've ever seen! Do you understand me, Graham Burton?"

A couple of men were hustling from the direction of the barn to see what all the yelling was about. Jackie didn't even notice them.

"Everywhere you go," she went on, they'll be

staring at your crotch, from grocery checkers to the Junior League, all of 'em wondering about your *problem*. I'll make you more famous than Kelsey's stud bull—and people think he's somethin' from outer space!"

With an unwilling bark of laughter, Gray threw up his hands in mock defense. Then he grabbed her, dragged her to the front steps, and sat her down hard on the top one. His hand clamped around her shoulders as he sat beside her.

She was still a wildcat, and she still made him laugh.

"Now, Jack . . ." he started, then coughed to disguise his laughter. "Premature *what*?"

Jackie⁻ squirmed around to blast him again. That was when she saw her classic '59 Rambler rolling toward the stone wishing well in the center of the circular drive.

"No!" She jerked up and tried to run, but the man had arms like steel tentacles, and he was just as determined that she was going to stay right there. "My car!" she wailed, straining against him. Gray finally saw what she did, just before the car hit the well with the sound of grinding metal.

Gray let her go, and Jackie stood and started forward in slow, slow motion. Quiet filled the air. The stone-and-mortar wishing well didn't show a scratch, but the right front end of her car was crushed into the tire like crumpled paper.

Men were all around them now, and even Merle had come out from the house.

It couldn't get any worse, Jackie thought. She'd lost her husband, her father, and now her car.

That car was such a large part of her history, her first burst of independence.

Gray saw her face and reached for her elbow. As soon as he touched her, she jerked away.

When she spoke, her voice was soft. "From the moment you walked into that bar last night, my life's been one nasty mess after another. I thought I was past all that." She looked down and dragged in a breath. "Yesterday I had a job, a car, and a modest income. Now I've got no money, no job, and no gas. But that's okay . . . because *I don't have a car.*" She stared at him. "Do you have to ruin everything you touch?" With a defiant shake of her head, she held back a sob. "Just stay out of my life."

She stepped forward with what she hoped was great dignity, reached in the side window that wouldn't close for her purse, and walked away.

About five hundred feet down the highway she heard the truck behind her, grinding gears. She didn't bother to look, she knew who it was.

"You gonna walk all the way home?" he called out the window to her.

"That's right." Her voice was just as crisp as she could make it.

"Come on, Jacqueline." His voice, on the other hand, was low and coaxing. "It's too hot to walk."

She didn't answer. Far down the highway, the horizon sizzled and spread into a thin mirage.

He drove alongside her for a few feet more before pulling ahead to park across the shoulder. He opened the truck door, waiting for her.

Jackie planned to walk around it, until she saw that he was still barefoot. One big toe was bleeding. He hadn't even taken the time to pull on his boots.

Very uncowboylike, she mused. Gray was frowning and looked frustrated. She spared him a puzzled glance. What did he care?

"Now, Jack. You know we need to talk. We haven't seen each other in years. Besides, I swore to Merle I'd bring you back. You don't know her, but she'll beat my butt if I show up without you."

Jackie threw her head back, hoping she looked tough, "No sale, Junior."

"Dammit." Gray was getting exasperated. She looked so fragile. "Listen, I want to talk to you, and it looks like you're in some kind of bind because of me."

"Forget it."

They stared at each other until he rubbed the back of his neck and mumbled, "Maybe I was . . . sort of rough on you back there."

He waited, wondering if she realized what she'd called him. He'd been "Junior" since their first date, when she'd told him she didn't want him to feel he was too old for her. He would have resented it from anyone else, but not from Jack. Even now, it felt right to have her call him by a name no one else could use.

It was tempting, Jackie thought, despite what had passed between them. She was so tired, tired of the aloneness of her own thoughts and the decisions that had to be made to straighten out her life. It didn't have to change anything if she just talked to him for a few minutes and then he took her home, did it? She looked again at his bare feet and thought about the blister she already had from work. It was a long walk home.

"Come on, will ya?" he said. "Have a heart. I feel like hell. Don't make me chase you all the way home."

Her smile was pained because she could not believe she was actually walking around to the passenger door—or that his most convincing argument had been telling her that he felt like hell. As she reached for the handle, he pushed the door open.

"I don't have a single idea why I'm doing this," she said, glaring at him.

Grinning with satisfaction, he turned the truck around.

Jackie eyed Gray warily as Merle poured them both more coffee. She'd told them about the call she'd gotten from the sheriff about her dad's death, then about the events of the previous evening, carefully omitting the moments she had spent on Gray's bed.

"So, what are your plans?" Merle asked.

Jackie looked down at her cup. "I was going to make some quick cash, enough to keep my dad's ranch going for a while. I've gotten a couple of offers for the land, but . . ." She shook her head. "I just don't know."

"Can't wait to hightail it back to the action, huh?" Gray said, his tone implying she'd be giving in to sin.

"It's none of your business what I do, Graham." She tried to stare him down. "But for your information, I can make a living in the city. We don't all have million-dollar ranches to support us. I've got an instructor's job at the University of Houston, and I worked damned hard for it. What am I gonna do here, call myself Velvet and raise horses?"

"Your dad liked it fine enough," Gray said.

Jackie swallowed, waiting a moment before saying, "That's right. He did."

"And you'd rather work places like the Lone Star?" His blue eyes were cold.

"Yeah, I'm funny that way. I like to eat." She pushed back her chair with a loud scrape, holding her temper by a thread. "Damn you anyway, Graham Almighty Burton. You have no right to judge me or anything I do. *You* were the worst mistake I ever made! And I'm gettin' out of here."

"Wait . . . please." His hand shot out and grabbed her wrist in a grip she couldn't have broken if she tried. "Look, Jack, I'm sorry." He looked everywhere but at her. "I need about ten more hours sleep, and I'm taking it out on you. This isn't that easy, you know." His eyes warmed to turquoise. "Come on. Sit down, please?"

Merle filled the silence as the two stared at each other. "This heat's making everybody jumpy as an old dog on a full moon. Can't take nothin' serious."

"All I want is a ride home," Jackie said. She sat back down, still preoccupied by the big tanned hand wrapped around her wrist. The heat from his fingers had dangerously loosened her knees, and she didn't like it. He let her go to brush a long finger over the bruise on her jaw.

"Hank Turner is definitely due a visit," he said grimly.

Jackie looked down, trying to hide her reaction to that simple touch.

"Now, Gray," Merle said in alarm. "You just leave this to the police."

"Hmm."

"Don't you make that noise at me." Merle smacked her mug down on the table. "I know what that noise means . . . trouble! You just remember your father doesn't need the excitement."

"Dusty lives for excitement," Gray corrected her dryly.

"What he needs," Merle said, getting up abruptly, "is peace and quiet to recuperate. And you"—she gave him a pointed look—"are going to help me see that he gets it."

Jackie watched them, her gaze shifting between

them. She waited for the winner as tension filled the air. Then Gray turned to her.

She glanced nervously to the right and found Merle staring at her just as thoughtfully.

"We do need a cook." Gray rested his chin on his hand with the kind of casualness that was immediately suspect. "You'd really be doing us a favor."

"That's right." Merle seized the idea. "You surely would. It's just plain cooking—fried chicken, shepherd's pie, chili and fixins. I'll take care of what Dusty needs."

"Wanna job?" Gray asked.

"No thanks," Jackie said firmly.

"What's the matter? You need a job, so it must be me." He leaned back in his chair, his eyes half-closed, and grinned. "You afraid to be around me, Jack? Afraid you're still carryin' a torch?"

She threw her head back. "Honey, you were just a bad case of measles. Somethin' that ruins your life for a while but doesn't end up leaving much of an impression. No, I'm not afraid to be near your manly self."

"Ooh-hoo!" Merle fanned her face with her napkin. "Shot you down, boy!"

"All right then," he said. "To the Circle B's new cook!" He raised his cup.

Jackie looked at both of them. "But . . . but what about Merle . . . ?" she sputtered, desperate for a way out.

"See, it's like this, sugar." Merle sat back down. "Gray's dad, well he's been in the hospital—got careless playin' with that pet bull of his." Jackie's eyes widened with concern. "Gored him right in the stomach," Merle went on. "Dusty was three hours in surgery. But he's gonnna be fine. Ben's stayin' up in Houston, keepin' him company. Now, anybody else would be sensible and take a little time to recover, take it easy. But the man's a yeller about everything that doesn't matter, holds in everything else. Left to himself, he'll pull out every stitch and bleed to death."

Merle caught herself before she got any more carried away with her favorite gripe. "Anyway, he's comin' home this week, but he's gonna need someone to tie him to his bed, watch his diet, and keep him occupied. The man's terr'ble when he's sick—a lot like this one." She laughed at Gray's bland expression. "I was a registered nurse before I took this job—still patch up the boys when they get hurt around here. Besides, Dusty needs somebody with a thick hide to take his lip. Thing is, that leaves the boys without a full-time cook."

"And you're looking for a job," Gray added.

"Pay's good." Merle looked meaningfully at Gray. "You'd only be feeding the family for breakfast and dinner. Then at lunch, you cook for ten. I'd still have plenty of time to do most of the housekeepin'. Half day Saturday and then Sundays off. We could use you for the whole summer."

It was tempting, very tempting. Best offer she'd get around here. Then Jackie remembered. "No, I can't . . . the hours. Who'd take care of my ranch?"

Merle was having no excuses. "Well, you'd probably want to stay here, and that way"—her eyes flashed brightly with inspiration—"you could rent your place for the summer. Give your tenant a break for caring for your stock. Gray, isn't Rand Holden looking for a rental for a few months for him and Jenny while they find a house?"

"Um-hmm," Gray stretched out his long legs, looking pleased with himself as he let Merle bull-doze ahead.

"Couldn't find a better man for horses," Merle

said. Obviously it was all settled in her mind. "And Jenny keeps a house spit shinin'."

"We really do need somebody," Gray said "You take the job and"—he threw in the clincher—"I'll make sure your car gets fixed."

Jackie bit her bottom lip. That sad old heap was a weakness, and he had zeroed right in on it. It had been her sixteenth birthday present from her dad. It ate parts for breakfast and had probably supplied her mechanic with a Swiss bank account, but she loved it like a pet and Gray knew it. Besides, where could she work in this town without transportation?

She considered the angles, trying to make up her mind as fast as they were making propositions. An old flare of excitement ran through her at the thought of seeing Graham every day. The truth was, they'd never be able to stay out of each other's way, and it might be terrible. But she could take it if he could.

And, if she rented her ranch out, she might be able to get some bills out of the way. She might even be able to keep it after all. There was really only Lucy to worry about, and it wasn't for that long. The other horses could be handled by any good ranch hand.

She only hoped she wasn't doing this just to be near him.

"I've got a mare in foal I need to look after," she said. "Could I stable her here? You can deduct feed and board."

"Sure thing," Gray said, before Merle could. Jackie looked so proud, so young. Her eyes seemed to pull him in, even though they had a wary gleam he'd like to wipe away.

He'd thought about her more than he cared to remember over the years, wondering how she was, what she was doing. She'd been such a kid when they got married.

He'd taken her on the rodeo circuit with him, both of them full of rebellion against their parents. He hadn't been any prize. He'd been his own boss for the first time in his life, and he'd liked it. He'd liked the danger of riding bulls, of being a celebrity and having money that came from his own sweat. What he hadn't liked was the cowboys who wanted his sweet, pretty wife.

"If I do this," Jackie said, bringing him back to the present, "I'll be on my own in the kitchen. I won't be treated like a helpless idiot or a child who needs to be told what to do."

He frowned indignantly. "I never treated you—"

"And," she interrupted him, "I won't bicker with you about the past."

His frown darkened. "Agreed," he said in a taut voice.

"All right then, for the summer." Jackie spoke quickly before she changed her mind. Though she didn't have a whole lot of choice right now. "When do I start?"

Merle beamed. Gray stood and announced, "I guess I'll go have a look at what's holdin' up that old well."

Three

Jackie was settling things at her house, readying it for her tenants, when grizzled Buck Brady paid her a call. He wouldn't come in, but stood on her porch, hat in hand, and explained that her father had given him a loan, a handshake deal. In return, Buck owed her two hundred of his finest Angus, which he was taking care of for her in his south pasture.

Jackie was stunned. It could make all the difference.

After Buck left, she paid a visit to the bank. Things might be manageable after all. The ranch account would be released in her name in another week, she was told, and there was enough to support the ranch for six weeks, even if she did nothing else.

She borrowed Buck's rig to move Lucy to the Burton barn and slept easier that night than she had in weeks. She woke sometime before dawn the next morning, the morning that Gray was coming to get her.

Trying not to think too closely about what she

was doing, about the fantasy she was allowing to guide her actions, she had cleaned and organized. She knew she was tired of being alone, and she still envied Gray because he *belonged* somewhere. He had a life he had chosen, family, money. Maybe if she worked there a while she would stop romanticizing about what might have been. But Gray seemed different, as if the wild, reckless streak he'd had when they were married had finally, somehow, been satisfied.

Still, he was so much like what she had imagined he would turn out to be. She felt as if this were a game she had begun that needed completion.

Jackie shook her head as she closed a filled cardboard box. They'd been divorced for years, and for good reason. Besides, neither he nor Merle had even mentioned Tom.

She started on another box. This couldn't be healthy.

She had stayed in Gray's thoughts for days; her straight back and the vulnerable curve of her mouth. It was crazy how she still made him want her, still made him want to protect her. Merle had been drawn to her, too, anxious to do something to help.

Jack had always had that quality. The first time they ever really met, he'd been driving the backroads in his daddy's truck. One minute he was squealing around a curve, the next he nearly crashed into her beat-up old Rambler stuck on the side of the road. An unmistakably feminine backside was visible as she bent over, reaching into the engine.

He made a fast U-turn and pulled up in front of her.

She straightened, and he grinned at the sweet-faced blonde. She had a grease spot on her nose and too tight jeans.

She smiled back, brushing her hands over her hips. "Well, it's not the carburetor." She blushed. "Know anything about dinosaurs?"

That made him laugh.

"I'll take a look," he said, still eyeing her. If it had an engine, he could make it go.

She'd been eighteen, much too young for him, but she was different from the other girls he knew. There was nothing bored or pampered about Jack, and nothing coy. She was real; grease-smudged, digging-in-an-engine, laughing-eyed real.

He'd fallen hard and fast.

Still remembering that day, Gray drove over to the Stone place to fetch Jack. He hadn't been there in years, and what he saw when he pulled up the drive was what his own ranch might look like if no one put a hand to it for months or money into it for years. The two-story house rambled back and to the left. Familiar outdoor scents drifted on a light breeze as he looked around. The yard needed mowing, but that wasn't what gave the place such a feeling of sadness.

It was something in the air—a kind of quiet.

The front screen door whined open and hit the side of the house with a loud thwack. And there she stood, her cat's eyes unreadable, her skin creamy looking. Her golden hair was piled high on top of her head, and the tails of the man's plaid shirt she wore were tied at her waist. It wasn't his.

His gaze lingered at the exposed triangle of pale skin before drifting down over ragged cutoffs to her bare legs. Bare legs he remembered wrapped around him as she sighed and cried and called his name.

One of the thin ties from her sandals was slipping, but he didn't tell her. He liked it.

He let his gaze roam back up as she braced herself on each side of the doorway, leaning forward. He wondered if she was consciously being provocative. Knowing Jack, he doubted it. His body went right into high gear anyway.

"It's all packed up," she announced, a trace of sadness in her voice. "I just have to move a couple of boxes. Come on in."

He nodded. "Okay."

She watched him, fascinated despite her intentions. Every move he made was smoother, more fluid than she remembered. He got out of the truck and slammed the door. In a black T-shirt and jeans, he looked like a cowboy—sleek and tough and cocky.

A lock of sandy hair fell over his forehead as he tipped his hat back. He squinted against the white glare of the Texas sun.

He seemed to be waiting for something.

"Hot," she said self-consciously as she pushed a loose strand of her own hair back into place. She felt too much like she was onstage. He did that to her. "You wanna soda?"

"Sounds good." He finally started toward her.

Before he got too close, she led the way to the kitchen. Brightly colored calico curtains fluttered at the window over the wide sink. Well-used pots and pans hung in two rows.

"One thing we've always got is ice," she said lightly, then her cheeks reddened as she thought of all the things he would probably think she meant they didn't have. And there was no *we* anymore. Opening the door of the fridge, she buried her nose inside.

Gray turned around to glance at the living room, with its worn couch, her father's easy chair, and the scarred coffee table. He remembered sitting on that couch while her dad sat in the easy chair and smoked his pipe. Bill had made it quite clear that he thought Gray was too old and too wild for his eighteen-year-old daughter. But they had persisted and pestered him until he had finally allowed them to go out.

Six months later they had run off to get married, because they couldn't keep their hands off each other and Gray couldn't face the sneaking around anymore. He had been too possessive to let Jackie be free any longer. Some part of him was afraid he'd lose her.

The sound of running water invaded his memories, and his gaze returned to Jackie. She was filling a tin ice tray. When was the last time he'd seen a tin ice tray? he wondered.

"This'll be real nice for Rand and Jenny," he said. "They've been living in the trailer while they were looking for a place. Jenny'll love an honest-to-goodness kitchen. She's always talkin' about it." He drank half of the drink Jackie had fixed him, then finished it and set the glass on the drain board. "Good." He wiped the back of one hand across his mouth.

Jackie had to look away fast when he glanced up, but he caught her anyway.

"What's so funny?" he asked.

"Nothing." Her chest felt heavy, her breathing uneven.

He waited.

"It's just . . . well, this is all so strange, being here in this house with you . . . making conversation about Jenny and how she wants a kitchen."

He made a sound that might have been amusement and shrugged one shoulder. "Jenny was my chemistry partner at Jeff Davis. I remember how much trouble she got me into. She probably makes atomic brownies." The crow's feet were more pronounced as his eyes teased. "You got fire insurance?"

"I'll include it in the rent." She found it hard to resist the simple affection in his voice. She had sensed his affection for Merle too. In her own life, affection had never been simple. With Gray, least of all.

"You planning on selling this place, Jack?"

That startled her. "Depends," she said, looking away.

"On . . . ?"

"Things."

He let it go. "That's some mare you dropped on our doorstep."

She smiled fleetingly, but didn't answer. Finally he cleared his throat and reached into his shirt pocket.

"Um, I've got something of yours." He pulled out a handful of green bills.

Her head jerked up. "You went to the Lone Star."

He pushed the money across the counter to her. "It's your pay for the week. The tips you lost are in there too." When she didn't speak or move, he said, "It's your money."

She couldn't look at him. She reached for the bills, and her fingers carefully closed around them. She couldn't thank him. She wanted to, but she couldn't.

"I guess you didn't get hurt," she finally said.

"Not where you can see." He put a hand under his ribs and smiled ruefully.

"Did you get your money back?"

"Um-hmm."

"Thank you." There, she'd done it. An unaccustomed shyness overwhelmed her as she slipped the money into the pocket of her cutoffs.

Bending his head toward her, Gray filled his lungs with her scent. He remembered that too.

"You're welcome," he said.

"Why does Hank hate you so much?" she asked. She suddenly felt they were standing too close and took a small step away.

He didn't say anything for a minute, apparently trying to decide how much to tell her. Finally, he began, "It happened when we were in school. One night after a game I was the last one in the locker room. I was just about to leave when I heard a girl cry out. Hank had her behind the last row of lockers, pushed up against the wall. She was crying so hard, she could hardly speak, Jack. But she was crying for him to stop." He shrugged and his mouth twisted. "I . . . helped her out."

She could imagine what he didn't tell her. The scene was very clear.

"Hank didn't hit me." She bit her lip. "If you went after him because of me, I have to tell you he wasn't the one who hit me."

He stiffened. "Who did?"

"Why are you doing all this?" she asked abruptly.

"All what?"

"Why are you being so nice to me—giving me a job, fixing my car? All of it?" Her throat closed, and she looked away.

He gazed at her a long time without speaking, his face quite serious.

"You know," he said at last, "I've learned a few things since my rodeo days. I wasn't the easiest guy in the world to live with, maybe I deserved—"

"I won't explain myself to you, Graham," she interrupted fiercely. "You wouldn't listen to me then, and I won't talk about it now.'

He looked at her long and hard before he finally said, "I understand." What was there to explain? he asked himself. He simply hadn't been able to hold her. He frowned and gritted his teeth. But she was here now, and she was still attracted to him. And he sure as hell still wanted her. Maybe he was lying to himself. Maybe the truth was that he wouldn't mind getting a little of his own back in exchange for debt; the loss of a wife, the loss of a brother.

He changed the subject. There was something else he did want to hear. "Who hit you, Jack?" he asked softly.

Jackie looked at him, then away, wondering how to get out of answering.

His hand lifted to her face, and one finger caressed the length of her jaw. "Who, honey?"

"It doesn't matter. Really."

Gray had the strangest impression that this fragile-looking woman was trying to protect him. It felt so good that he thought he might just let her, for a while. "Well, I guess I could move those boxes."

"That's okay." Her eyes met his before she turned away. "I can do it. It'll just take a minute. They're in here."

"Here" was her father's bedroom. The bed was stripped down to the mattress. There wasn't much else to the room—a TV and a dresser with a mirror above it.

"I used to see Bill at the stock shows," Gray said

quietly. "I remember one night we went out drinking after." He laughed at the look she gave him. "Yeah, we did. He outbid me on a filly, and he wanted to make sure I knew it wasn't personal."

Jackie smiled. Her dad had always liked Gray.

His voice was gentle when he added, "Sorry he had to go that way, Jack."

She shrugged and tightened her lips. "Nothing anybody could do."

Three boxes sat on the floor next to the empty closet. A picture of Jackie at fourteen poked out of one of them.

Gray reached for it. "Cute kid. Sassy."

She snatched it back, gave a noncommittal "Hmm," then hunched down to stuff it back into the box.

"Still is." He bent to lift the box and grinned right into her face. She bounced up and stepped back too quickly, almost tripping.

"Careful there," he said casually. "Where do you want this?"

"In the attic." She tried to regain her composure as she walked ahead through the hall to open the attic door.

Fifteen minutes more and they were on their way, with Jackie's two suitcases in the back. Gray was quiet, as if he knew how hard it was for her to leave and didn't want to intrude on her thoughts. As they drove up to the Burton ranch, she saw they had towed her car somewhere out of sight. The wishing well stood like a stone beacon in the center of the drive.

"It's a beautiful place," she said as he turned off the ignition. She couldn't help comparing it to her own.

"Yeah," he said, looking around. "It's taken a lot of years of Dusty's blood and sweat."

She looked at him in surprise. When she'd known Gray, he'd resented the fact that Dusty had given everything he was to the ranch. Now, he sounded as if he admired him for it.

When she started to grab one of the heavy cases, Gray took it away from her, shaking his head in mock exasperation. They were twice as big as she was.

"Just get the door," he said.

"I can do it myself." She looked mutinous, but he wasn't going to wait around for the fight. He forged ahead. Not to be outdone, Jackie ran to throw open the screen with what might be considered unnecessary force.

"Key's over the door," he said.

She reached up, her hand groping across the top of the door frame. She made an almost unbearably provocative picture, straining on tiptoe in those tight cutoffs, her blond hair swinging.

"The door, Jack?" He counted on the sarcasm to distract him.

Her head jerked around and her lips compressed, but she found the key and inserted it in the lock without another word. Then she pushed the door open with her own sarcastic flourish.

He strode in, then stopped at the bottom of the stairs.

"Merle went to pick up Pop. Ben'll be coming back tonight too." He saw how Jackie stood just inside the door, looking a bit lost. "Come on." He tilted his head toward the stairs, "You won't recognize the place."

She followed him up the stairs, her eyes scanning the pictures that splashed the wall. In the upstairs hall there were more, of all the boys. Grade school, Little League, high school. A few were with their mother and father, who stood with their hands on the boys' shoulders, everyone's hair perfectly in place. It was all too familiar. She hurried to catch up to Gray.

"Merle's got my old room," he said. "Dusty let her redecorate a couple years ago." He pushed open a door with his foot. "She calls this the blue room."

It certainly was blue . . . and grand. A giant four-poster dominated the room, and the floor was covered in a blue-and-off-white Oriental rug with peach flowers. Someone had placed a bunch of wildflowers on a small desk near the window.

"It's nice," she said as Gray put down one suitcase and lifted the other onto the bed. She didn't know what else to say that wouldn't sound as if she'd never slept before in a room that looked like it belonged in a French chateau. Her throat tightened, and she got angry at herself for being overwhelmed by Burton wealth . . . again.

"Bathroom's in the hall where it always was." He nodded to his left. "Well, I better be getting back to work." He gave an awkward shrug. This was harder than he thought it would be.

Jackie followed him down the stairs. "Thanks for the ride."

"Sure." He smiled at her over his shoulder.

"And for getting my money from Hank." They were at the porch now. She was on her way to the barn, anyway, she told herself.

"My pleasure," he called out as he climbed into the truck. "Just make yourself at home. They'll be back in a little while. Merle said to tell you not to worry about dinner, she's taken care of everything." He started the truck, then leaned across to the passenger window to say something else. Jackie had to bend at the waist to see him. "Hmm,

Jack. There's just one other thing I think you should know."

"What is it?" She bent lower.

"I, uh, lied to you."

"What?" She was startled. "What are you talking about?" She raised her hand to shade her eyes and watched that slow, lazy grin come.

"The other day in the kitchen, I lied. I did remember more than just the face."

Then he gunned the motor and drove off with a cloud of dirt, leaving Jackie standing bent over at the waist, one hand covering her mouth.

Merle got home around five with Dusty and Ben. It was quite a production. Jackie heard the motor from upstairs and came out to the porch. The car was the same old Lincoln they'd had for a million years. She could hear the sound of an argument through the closed windows before two of the doors flew open.

Merle jumped out of the front seat, scolding. "Dudn't matter what you say, old man. You are gonna do just what Ah tell you. No choice. No choice at all."

Ben got out from the driver's side and walked around the car. He must be about twenty now, Jackie thought, so grown-up since she had seen him last. He was tall, nice looking. She watched as he opened the door to the backseat while Merle was still lecturing. She was touched by the amount of care Ben used to help his father out of the car.

The family resemblance was strong between them. All the Burtons had the same coloring and, it seemed, the same temperament.

"I got a choice, I got all kindsa choice!" Dusty

shouted. His voice was deep and scratchy, like he'd swallowed sand. "I can fire you, that's what!"

"Well ain't that too bad, 'cause Ah don't fire!" Merle's voice cracked as she laughed. "After the last time, Ah decided Ah jus' can't be bothered payin' attention to your big talk. So now you go stick that in your pipe!"

"Woman, there's more aggravation in you than one man can stand, bossin' ever'body this way and that. I can walk!" He batted his son's hands away and straightened, obviously in pain. He might have been Gray at sixty, a little fuller around the middle, and with a hundred more creases in his tanned face, but the cool gemstone eyes were the same, as was the light brown hair.

"Come on, Pop," Ben coaxed, "you don't want to pull those stitches. One of the interns told me Merle bribed 'em to write her initials in catgut." While he talked, Ben's arm encircled his father's waist and he walked him forward a few steps.

"Ah never did, Benjamin Burton!" Merle exclaimed as Dusty laughed a low whiskey laugh. When they finally got closer to the porch, Dusty looked up and saw Jackie standing there.

"Well, hello, purty thing," he drawled. "Long time, ain't it?" Then he grinned his "Dusty" grin and held out his arms.

Never in her life would she be able to resist the open arms of this Burton. She ran into his embrace, and he whispered in her hair, "Good to have you here, darlin'."

When they finally pulled away from each other, both their eyes were watery. Dusty cleared his throat. "Merle told me you were gonna help us out for a few months. Obliged to ya, little girl."

She was charmed, completely, as Dusty had

always charmed her. *Little girl.* It was a speech her own dad might have made.

"All right, you old buzzard," she said, hiding a knowing smile. "Stop workin' me. I'm here only 'cause I need some dough and your son cost me my job." She wagged her finger. "And it's only for the summer."

"Hee-yah!" Dusty whooped, though it was just short of a cough. "This is gonna be good. I do love fireworks!"

Merle smirked. "Ah'm warnin' you now, girl. Don't let him butter you up or you'll be right under his thumb with the rest of us."

"Under my thumb," Dusty muttered disgustedly. "Get me to bed, boy. I can't wait to start givin' this mean woman orders!"

"Just a minute, Pop." Ben grinned shyly at Jackie and held out his own arms for a hug. "I haven't said hello to Jackie yet. C'mere, you."

She went into his arms as easily as she had Dusty's. "You've grown up so much, I hardly know you," she said.

"And you're single!" he joked.

Jackie couldn't take that as a joke. She froze, and he realized his mistake just as quickly.

Stiff with embarrassment, they pulled apart. Eyes averted, Jackie strode up the steps and held open the screen door.

As the other three followed, she could see the strain on Dusty's face, but he just gritted his teeth and kept going. They had reached the porch when Gray's green pickup came up the drive and around the circle, spitting gravel. She couldn't stop the betraying flush that tinted her cheeks.

"Pop!" Gray's smile was dazzling as he jumped out of the truck. "You're early. What'dya do, run all the way?" Up the porch steps in one leap, he put an arm around Dusty's shoulders and gave him a squeeze. He scanned his father's face, then glanced at Ben. Ben shrugged helplessly.

"You look good, Pop." Gray stepped back and gestured for Ben to take Dusty through the door.

"Boy, you're the worst liar in three counties," Dusty said. "I know just what I look like. But I'll be ridin' fence in a week. So you watch out, I might steal this purty thing right out from under your nose." He winked back at her, and Jackie blushed again.

What did he mean by that? she wondered a moment later. Did he think Gray and she—?

By the time she came out of it, she was the last one on the porch, still holding open the screen door. Gray's head poked back out.

"You coming in, Jack?"

"*What* did you tell your father about me," she whispered fiercely, "about why I'm here?"

"I didn't get a chance to say anything," he mock-whispered back. "Merle did the honors."

"He thinks we're together, doesn't he!" She clutched his arm, pulling him back outside.

"Naw. You're in his house, I'm in my house."

"He does, I can tell!"

"So? It'll give him something to think about. Keep his mind off the pain." That lazy grin was back, teasing her.

"I want you to go in there and tell them I'm not—that we're not—" Her arms slashed the air.

"Okay," He shrugged and started back inside.

"No, wait!" Suspicious, she grabbed his arm again. She could feel his muscles bunch beneath her fingers. "What are you going to say?"

"I'll say, 'Now, Pop, I'll have you know that purty girl is *not* sleeping with me, and I am shocked that you could think so.' How's that?"

She wanted to scream so badly, but her teeth wouldn't unclench. "That'll just make it worse, and you know it! They'll think we're covering up!"

"Well, you tell me what to say, then, Jack," he said with exaggerated patience as he slipped his thumbs in his belt loops, slouching back against the door frame.

She opened her mouth and couldn't think of anything. He looked so innocent, she wanted to hit his other eye. Setting her shoulders and ignoring that laughing glint, she stepped right by him and on into the house.

Four

What *was* that sound?

One of Jackie's hands ventured out from beneath the mound of covers, waving back and forth like a drunken sea gull. On the third pass, it landed on the phone, knocking the receiver from its cradle. Inching sideways, her fingers slapped at the alarm button. Blessed silence followed.

Arm still outstretched, Jackie moaned into the pillow. Seconds passed. Gathering momentum, she threw off the covers and landed on her back with a great whoosh of air. One eye opened, then the other.

Dark. It was pitch black.

Slowly rolling her head in the direction of the clock, she tried to focus on the fuzzy dial. Four . . . uhh . . . thirty.

Her eyes closed tight.

Jackie didn't much care for morning—any morning.

Raising herself by inches, she finally managed to drag her poor body out of bed and propel it forward, hauling her robe behind her.

Twenty minutes later, the coffee was started, the table set, and the sausage was cooking. She could do this, she thought. The only thing she worried about was portions. How much could they eat?

Well, pancakes to start. She could fill up a dump truck with pancakes.

She was mixing batter when Gray came in from outside, shiny clean, his hair still wet. Buttoning the last button on his shirt, he walked in with his head down.

"Good morning," she said, wishing her voice had more *umph*. How the devil could just the sight of him do that to her pulse, her senses?

His sleepy gaze roamed over her in welcome. "Mornin'." His voice was rough around the edges, an intimate sound, warming her all out of proportion. So many mornings they had forgotten everything to love each other till noon.

Gray had been insatiable and so had she. Even when things got bad and they hardly spoke to each other, that wild hunger had held them together.

Suddenly uncomfortable, she turned back to the stove, making a great business of pouring batter.

Gray got himself a cup of coffee and growled his satisfaction at the taste. Leaning against the counter next to her, he watched her work.

"Find everything okay?" he asked.

She glanced at him. "Sure. Merle showed me last night." She could feel the tension building, but she was helpless to stop it. She pretended not to notice instead, flipped the pancakes, and went to the fridge for butter and juice. "Want some OJ?"

"Hmm." Gray kept watching her. He wanted her

so badly, he could feel the curve of her backside in the palm of his hand. She set the butter and juice on the table, then stepped back to the stove, shoveled the cakes out of the pan and into the warming oven, and started two new ones. He stood just out of her way, sipping coffee, hard as a rock.

"Can you reach that?" She looked expectantly at the syrup on the third shelf of the cabinet above her.

"Yep." He put his mug down on the counter and cornered her as he reached up above her for the large plastic bottle. He leaned lightly against her, and an alarm went off in Jackie's head.

Uh-uh. No, you don't, she told herself. You're not going to start that, Jackie Stone. It's not you and him—it's just him. He turns it on and off like a faucet.

When his arm came down, it came down slowly and deliberately. He smelled soapy and warm, with a man scent that was as familiar as her own, though it shouldn't be. He placed the bottle on the counter, and she felt his breath stir her hair. Finally, he moved away.

"Quit pickin' on me," she said, giving him a sideways look.

He grinned. "Who, me?"

She turned away with her best businesslike manner.

"Hey," he said quietly, and she looked back by reflex. Before he could go on, they heard the sound of boots coming down the stairs.

"Smells great!" Ben stormed in, filling the room with his live-wire energy. "Hey, Gray, Jackie." He grinned happily, looking toward the stove. "All right! Pancakes!"

Merle walked in behind him. "Dusty's still

asleep. Looks like you're doin' fine, Jackie. Need a hand?"

"Oh, no, just help yourself to coffee."

It was rather like being a Little League coach mistakenly given a chance at the majors, Jackie thought as she set the pancakes on the table. The Burton men knew all there was to know about eating. They ate with an enthusiasm that bordered on passion and a kind of single-mindedness that had to be admired. And they certainly packed away enough to qualify as a team.

Ben hardly looked up. He just wolfed down his food, then pushed at his plate and waited. Gray had refined his talent somewhat for company. He cleaned his plate, then asked very nicely if there was more. Again and again.

Jackie kept looking over her shoulder from the stove, trying to judge the number of innings.

When they finally cleared out—after bestowing on her smiles that somehow made up for all the trouble—Merle rested both elbows on the table and laughed out loud.

"So, you still game?" she asked, licking at a bit of syrup on her thumb.

Horrified, Jackie laughed back. "I forgot what they're like. How could I forget how much they eat?"

"Mercy blackout."

"Somebody save me, ten of them for lunch!"

"Merle!" They both jumped when they heard Dusty holler.

"I'm comin', you old bear!" Merle hollered back, and started on her way.

While the chili cooked in two giant pots, corn bread baked in the oven and Jackie made a quick trip to the barn to see Lucy. The cathedral ceiling turned the light to fairest gold, and the odors of animals and earth peppered the air. Rustlings and whinnies followed her as she walked past the stalls.

Some of them looked freshly painted. She counted four down on the right, and there she was. Hollywood Lucy was a palomino cutting horse with beautiful conformation and the rounded belly that proved she would soon foal.

If Jackie's dad had had anything of worth, it was this mare.

"There's my girl," she said as she let herself into the stall. "What a beauty you are." Her hands slid over the sleek coat, and Lucy whickered softly at the familiar voice and touch. Jackie pulled an apple from her pocket and let the mare take it. "I bet you want a good rub, don't you, girl?"

"That's a fine mare you've got there."

Jackie whirled around, nearly losing her balance, to find a smiling, red-haired man leaning over one side of the stall. He touched his hat.

"Paddy O'Malley, miss." He was in his early fifties. His eyes were green, his face round and sunburned.

She nodded back. "Jackie Stone."

"A pleasure. The boss tells me to be sure and give ye whatever ye wish."

That surprised her. "That's very kind of you, Mr. O'Malley."

He grinned. "Just call me Paddy, miss. No ceremony. I pretty much have care of the stables. So if you have questions or complaints . . ."

"All right, Paddy." She smiled back. "Maybe you can show me through the tack room."

"Yes, miss." He slipped his hat back. "That would be right this way."

They started toward the back of the barn, but Jackie stopped at the next stall. "It's Poco!" She couldn't resist reaching out for Gray's horse. "That's my lovely fella," she cooed, slipping the stall open. Poco nodded his head way up and down, snorting in recognition, and Jackie searched her pockets for more sugar. "Here you go, old man," she murmured as he snuffled her palm. Her eyes filled with tears as she stroked his soft nose, and he raised his head to sniff at her hair, her neck.

She glanced back at Paddy, hoping he wasn't too impatient. He was leaning on the gate, smiling his approval.

That first lunch, a wild crowd of hungry men, Gray included, burst through the back door and elbowed their way to the bathroom for a quick wash.

During the few weekends Jackie had actually spent at the ranch, Gray had breakfasted hours before she'd gotten out of bed. She would take him lunch, and they had eaten, or not eaten, together. She didn't think she'd ever been present at one of these group "feeds."

She steeled herself now, glad for the bathroom's paper towel rack and double sinks. As they trickled back out, they introduced themselves, their eyes taking close inventory of her. After the third such tour of her body, Jackie reached for the butcher's apron and tied it on with fumbling fingers.

Evidently, somebody had kept a lid on who she was and what her name had once been. But that wouldn't last long.

"So they finally learned what a cowhand likes for lunch . . ." one said.

"Merlie," another exclaimed, "how you've changed!"

"That chili I smell? Wait, be still my heart—ah, roses!"

Jackie almost thought the flirting might interfere with their eating, but she soon realized there was no real possibility of that.

She'd made chili and corn bread for fifty and buckets of iced tea. "The boys" were quickly distracted. When she pulled out the bin of still warm Toll-House cookies, they loosed a new chorus of cowboy whoops.

"Hey, that was great!"

"I'd do anything for a woman 'can make a cherry pie."

"But d'ye make an Irish stew, miss?" Paddy asked, a twinkle in his eye. "I'm looking for me third wife."

"I can and I do, Mr. O'Malley," she teased him back. "But have a cookie instead. Wives are expensive." She laughed and tossed one high. Paddy caught it with one smooth swipe and gave her a nod of appreciation.

Throughout the entire meal, Gray watched her, his own mouth shut. She knew his gaze hardly left her, and she was waiting for some smart comment.

It never came. He filed out with the rest. Ben was baiting him about a horse that didn't like him. He'd looked at every object in the room, and still bypassed her on the way out. She frowned as she tried to understand him.

She had told herself that this first group meal would show her if he'd changed. She'd promised herself she wouldn't revert back to her teenage self, but would be the person she'd worked so hard to become, whether he liked it or not. That person wasn't afraid of light jokes and camaraderie. That person didn't sit quietly in a corner so no one would think she was a flirt or a tease. So what did Gray's silence mean?

She put the thought from her mind as she surveyed the kitchen, which looked like it might have belonged to the seven dwarfs on a bad day. She took a deep breath about the time Merle pushed the kitchen door in, holding Dusty's tray.

Taking in the situation with an expert eye, she said, "Ah have a friend Ah think you just might like to meet." Putting the tray down smartly on the counter, she patted the shiny metal face of an oversized automatic dishwasher.

"This here's Charlie—my bestest and dearest bud. He came with the negotiations for my raise."

Jackie acknowledged the introduction with the raising of one pale brow. "Charlie, you're a good-lookin' son of a gun."

They came dragging in at six sharp, filling the kitchen with the scents of man and horse and sweat, and memories of her childhood. Ben mumbled something about getting a shower and headed down the hall.

Gray went right for the fridge. He grabbed a beer and poured back half the can before he surfaced, giving her an exhausted smile.

"Hey, purty girl," he said softly.

She had noted the way he favored his right side, but tried to appear indifferent. "You have a disagreement with a horse, cowboy?"

"Guilty." Once again, Gray couldn't stop looking at her. The change in her amazed him. Somehow, just being there had softened the shell she'd put up around herself. He'd even heard her laughing at one of Ben's jokes at lunch. He liked her easy smile better than he liked short skirts.

"Anything a good soak in Epsom salts won't cure?" she asked.

"Can I let you know?"

"Sure," she said as he limped out the back door. "I've always fancied drivin' an ambulance."

Jackie went for a swim in the pool that night. Her pale blue suit was old, but the high-cut leg gave her freedom for laps. Slipping into the sun-warmed water, she sighed away every care. Back-stroke, float, backstroke, float, and she murmured the names of the stars.

"That's Orion," a voice corrected her, and she slipped beneath the surface, startled and sputter-ing. Her feet reached down, and she stood in the shallow end as she wiped her eyes and face.

"How do you know which constellation I meant?" she asked, tossing her hair over her shoulder.

"You always got 'em backwards," Gray said. His eyes told her he remembered teaching her about the stars from the back of his pickup.

He stood at the side of the pool in black trunks that hugged his body, and she couldn't help but stare at the sight of him, legs parted, above her. He was more solid than she remembered, more width and muscle.

Her mouth went dry as her gaze followed the lines of his body.

That was just memory, she told herself as she forced her gaze away. He could only hurt her.

She waded out of the pool, up the three steps,

and Gray watched like a man enraptured. She was everything soft and feminine to him. Long gold hair sloped over one white shoulder to breasts whose hard nipples were outlined in stark detail.

He followed her shape down to her hips, her thighs, and shuddered. He almost groaned at the pain it caused. His restraint was shredding as he said roughly, "Get in the house, Jack."

He saw the shocked response in her eyes, then the understanding. Without a word, she was gone, leaving a tremor in the air around him.

In the week that followed Jackie fell into a routine.

She liked *the boys,* liked their hustle to get the job done, and she liked hearing their oohs and ahhs when she made something special. Every one of them had a sweet tooth.

They teased and flattered her, and she teased back. They made her feel at home in a way that was comforting. What she could hardly believe was Gray's lack of temper.

Oh, he watched her, and watched *the boys.* But he seemed to understand that it was all in fun, or maybe he was just keeping his feelings to himself. The word had long gotten around that she was Gray's ex-wife, and no one pushed the flirting too far. But it had never taken much to start Gray on that jealous horse before. Maybe he had changed, Jackie mused, or maybe he simply didn't care because she didn't belong to him anymore. But how would *she* know? She'd never understood him when they were together.

He told her over breakfast one morning that the ranch was now diversified, as a lot of modern

Texas ranches were. They raised both cattle and horses, and leased out a bit of land for oil. They had trained cutting horses for the last couple of years, since Gray had come home.

Every day, after she had taken care of her own chores, Jackie would find her way out to the corral. Sometimes she went to watch them work, sometimes she exercised Lucy.

Watching Gray one afternoon, she remembered why they'd called him "Grace" on the rodeo circuit. She loved the way he moved, whether it was catching a high fly in a Saturday baseball game or sitting atop a stallion determined to get him off. Actually, Gray did more coaxing than hard breaking.

He was breaking a chestnut mare this time. He walked her around with a hackamore, talking slow and easy. He blew into her nostrils and ran his hands over her chest and neck; he gave her sugar and small, teasing pieces of carrots and apples.

Jackie leaned on the fence as he laughed his low laugh and rubbed the heel of his hand between the mare's eyes. Then he winked at Jackie and started humming some sixties Motown tune as he scratched the place on the mare's back where he wanted to sit.

He slid a blanket and, at last, a saddle over her. After a time he walked her back to her stall. Jackie saw him through the kitchen window an hour later, starting all over again.

Jackie was used to the rough-and-tumble ways of rodeo cowboys who accepted nothing but complete surrender. Once, Gray had been one of them. It touched something in her to watch him, to see how different he'd become.

Two afternoons later he led a mare past her as

she leaned on the fence. "You wanna meet my kids?" he asked.

Startled, heart pounding, she straightened and nodded slowly.

"Well, come on, then." Gray grinned over his shoulder, enjoying watching the color wash her high cheekbones as she looked at him, then looked down. She tramped along the fence beside him until they were close to the stables. The corral was connected to the building at one end, and she had to climb over the fence to join him.

He waited for her, holding the reins of the skittish copper-colored mare. "This is Gypsy, out of Sidewalker."

With those words, Jackie realized his "kids" were his horses. She raised a hand to the mare's head, murmuring reassurances, and the mare quieted.

"You still got the touch, Jack," he said, curiously satisfied.

"She knows I think she's beautiful, that's all," Jackie said, gazing into the great, chocolate-brown eyes.

"Right."

Somehow, the mare's halter had changed hands, and Jackie was now leading her. Once inside the barn, Gray strode ahead to the section of newly painted stalls. Gypsy lipped sugar cubes from Jackie's palm as they walked. When they approached Gray, standing next to Gypsy's stall, he grinned and reached for her hand.

Jackie didn't think to pull away. Raising his knee, he wiped her palm dry on the soft denim stretched over his thigh. She gasped in shock as heat rocketed through her.

"She's a messy eater," he said.

It was just a simple gesture, but after she pulled her hand back, she couldn't meet his eyes.

He took her through the stalls, seeming not to notice her discomfort. There were ten horses in all, each one full of breeding and grace. With every introduction, he gave her the name of the sire or dam, whichever was better known.

She had to admit, he had an impressive lot, and he was papa proud of every one of them. And she wasn't jealous. Not too much. Maybe he had ten first-class animals and she only had one. Still, her father hadn't done badly. His horses weren't so far beneath Gray's. And just this one name foal could make her entire stable twenty times more valuable. Still, as she turned away, Jackie couldn't help wondering how different it would have been if she and Gray had stayed together.

Another week passed, and Jackie's days took on a comfortable pattern.

Every afternoon she spent time with Dusty, playing cards and listening to his stories. He still told the kind of ranch stories she liked best, of when he had first started out as a wildcatter, how he'd built the ranch to what it was, his favorite cutting horses over the years. He told her how gentle his bull, Max, really was. He'd raised Max from a calf, even ridden him, and he was as crazy for sugar as any horse and quite as gentle. He'd just been excited that day by the scent of a cow coming into her time.

When she had stayed at the ranch before, she hadn't seen that much of Dusty, or anyone else. Graham had been her whole world. Now, Dusty accepted her presence without a lot of questions. She beat him at gin three times out of five.

Once, he caught her watching Gray from his bedroom window when she was supposed to be working on a run of diamonds.

"Gray never did anything like anyone else," he said, grunting as he rearranged his position in bed. "He was different after you went away, crazy wild, then years older. He came and made peace with me, but he wouldn't stay here. Stayed on the circuit. We were glad when he finally decided to come home. Tom was always the steady one, Gray the rebel. Ben, the one with the soft heart."

"Where is Tom now, Dusty?" she asked as she sorted her cards.

He didn't answer. She felt tension cool the air and looked up to see Dusty's face the color of paste. She leaned forward.

"Gin," he said abruptly, throwing down his cards. He leaned back and stared up at the ceiling. "Guess I'm gettin' kinda tired, little girl. I won't hold this one against you. Maybe we can pick it up later on."

"Sure, Dusty." She gathered the cards and smoothed the covers. "You just yell out if you want anything." He made a small noise of assent, and she backed out, closing his door.

In the hallway she leaned against the wall and fanned the cards, her hands shaking. Just what she'd thought. Dusty hadn't had anything near gin.

Jackie was rarely in the kitchen when Merle wasn't in there with her. And she couldn't have picked a better friend. Merle's earthy humor kept Jackie from feeling lonely, and they talked about things Jackie hadn't talked about in years; town stories and scandals from long ago. Eventually they even talked a little about Gray.

"I guess you've heard talk about Gray and women after we split," Jackie hinted one day. She was helping Merle fold laundry, and it was Gray's worn denim work shirt she held in her hands. Even after washing, it held the scent of him.

"So?" Merle sorted socks as fast as she popped green beans. "You gonna hold them against him? Just because he never let any special girl break his heart again?"

"Where's Tom, Merle?" Jackie asked.

For once Merle had no bright answer. "Ah don't know, honey." She looked hard at the shirt she was smoothing, over and over. "Gray came home about three years ago. He and Tom fought about everything. After about a month, Tom announced that he was taking off for a job with one of the oil companies overseas. He sends postcards, but he travels a lot and he hasn't been home since." She made a sound that was almost a snort. "She-oot! How Gray could think a sweet thing like you and his own brother . . ."

Jackie stopped folding and stared at Merle, astonished. So, people still believed the gossip.

Merle laughed and shook her head. "Sorry, honey, I'm done. What's between the two of you is flat between the two of you. Ah ain't about to mess with it. Nope. Uh-uh." She laughed again. "Ah think Ah'm gonna make that old bear upstairs some pecan brownies. Soften him up for a little game of strip poker."

"Merle!"

"Jackie!"

Five

That same afternoon, Gray came into the kitchen and grinned at her until she finally had to stop cleaning up and face him, hands on hips.

"What?" She tilted her head, pretending to be out of patience.

He backed toward the front door, head down, still grinning. She dried her hands and followed. *The boys* were all lined up, like some kind of crazy honor guard, and they were waiting for her. When she stepped onto the front porch, the line began to part in the middle, with comic ceremony and great awkwardness, until a bit of pink showed through, then more.

There it stood, the monster she had called Baby since she was sixteen years old. But Baby had never shined like this. She looked like a museum piece.

Jackie raced down the steps. She ran a hand over the slick new paint from headlight to windshield. It had a new convertible top too.

One of the ranch hands clapped, then another, until they all joined in.

"Thank you," she whispered. She saw Gray and mouthed the words again before looking around for help.

Merle finally came to her rescue and bullied everybody into the kitchen for a snack. Gray stayed where he was, feet like lead, wondering why he felt so dumb.

By this time Jackie was hiding in the car, hands high on the wheel, face averted from him. He cautiously walked up to the car and bent down to look in the open window.

"You cryin', Jack?"

She didn't answer right away, but when she did she sounded mad. "So what?"

He knew she wasn't mad. "So . . . you wanna go for a ride?" He watched her face change, a half smile appear.

"Yeah, okay."

They only went as far as the west border of the ranch, and they didn't speak the whole time, but Jackie would always remember that ride.

The evenings were much cooler than the days, and Jackie took long walks after dinner. To her, there was nothing in the world like a Texas sunset. The colors were like a South Seas painting that changed moment to moment.

It was the time she liked best, when she let her mind wander back to her childhood memories, before her mother died. Even before Graham Burton, Jr.

She'd been so certain of everything when she was a teenager, certain she'd never make the mistakes her parents made, certain she'd be a perfect wife and mother of six. She'd have a husband who would bring her flowers and hold her in his arms every night. In her spare time, she would become famous for breeding the best cutting horses in Texas.

Some dreams die hard, but hers seemed just to slip away in the tough realities of every day.

Life on her daddy's ranch had been bittersweet, filled with everything she loved—her parents, all the animals—but there were so many "don't get too close" signs.

When she turned thirteen, her parents' fights became regular. They always fought over the same thing. Sometimes it was lipstick that triggered it, sometimes it was a story that somebody had told her mother about where they'd seen her dad . . . and with whom.

He was a good-looking man, and he thought a man just couldn't be tied down to one woman, not if he was a real man. He didn't even think he was supposed to be faithful. His own father, his uncles, and all his friends thought as he did.

Two years later when her mother died, everything changed. Her father seemed to think girls should take care of the house and the cooking and wear dresses with stiff petticoats. Jackie wanted to please him, she really did. But she couldn't seem to help herself. She'd sneak into the barn every chance she got, listening to tall tales from the hands about no-account broncs and silver buckles, riders who couldn't be thrown and golden bloodlines.

No job was too dirty or too hard for her, though she knew the hands spoiled her rotten. But she was doing what she wanted to do, learning as much about horses as she could absorb.

When she was sixteen, she started dating. She almost learned to hate her father then. He wanted to protect her from everything, and she was desperate to experience everything he wanted to protect her from. By the time she was eighteen, she was looking for trouble.

That was the year she finally met the great Graham Burton.

He was every girl's dream of a cowboy, with a hard body, a silver buckle, square jaw, and sweet talk. He took one look at her and made her feel that he was looking at a woman. He told her she was the prettiest thing he'd ever seen, that her eyes could drive a man out of his mind. He took her to her first bar where he taught her to drink tequila. On their fourth date he drove her up to Tumbledown Point and taught her why she should be glad to be female.

He made her feel grown-up, wicked, and so important. More important than she'd ever felt before. Best of all, he made her feel smart. He listened when she talked. They talked horses, and he took her opinions seriously. He even let her help him pick a colt at a stock show.

Jackie knew it was love.

At twenty-three, Gray was desperate to escape the cloud of being one of Dusty Burton's sons, the one named after him. He was wild about a yellow-haired girl. He was also rodeo crazy. When he decided to buy a battered horse trailer and follow the circuit, he asked Jackie to go with him, as his wife.

She had visions of sleeping under the stars, following the circuit from town to town in an exciting round of adventures.

And it was exciting, until the first time Gray got hurt. Three broken ribs and a cracked wrist. Jackie was so scared, she called her dad. He called Dusty, and suddenly the hospital was full of Burtons.

Gray was furious, and as soon as his family cleared out he laid into Jackie.

"Did he give you money?" he demanded in a tight voice.

Jackie knew he was proud, but she hadn't known what to do when Dusty had stormed into the hospital and taken charge. Now she didn't know how to tell Gray. "He paid the motel bill, and moved us down the street to the Ramada." She saw his teeth grind in his jaw, and warily added, "He paid the hospital too."

"Pay it back," Gray said flatly. "I don't care if it takes every cent we got, or if you have to sell the trailer, the truck, and Poco to do it."

She got the message loud and clear.

Things were better after that. Jackie got a job until Gray healed, and they got back on the circuit. They started saving for emergencies, but every time he got hurt Jackie worried herself sick about the bills.

Then Gray's older brother Tom joined the circuit. Those were the best times. They played poker and went dancing. Tom helped her get her GED. Everything would have been fine if she hadn't gotten pregnant.

She hadn't even known she was pregnant until she miscarried. She and Tom were out riding while Gray worked a pickup job at a local ranch. Suddenly she bent over the saddle with horrible cramps. Tom got her right to the hospital, but it was already too late.

She'd never forget the look on Gray's face when he found her crying in his brother's arms. She'd never forgive him his lack of trust.

When she left him, she couldn't face going back to Turbin and all the talk. She was sure her dad would say she should have stayed with Gray. So she moved to Houston, found a roommate, and got a job at the university.

It took her six years to get her bachelor's degree. When she finally called her father, she found he didn't blame her at all. The funny thing was, he never questioned her. He blamed Gray.

Even now she still shied away from relationships. But since that night at the Lone Star, she had felt a curious yielding within herself, a vague yearning she didn't want.

One evening Jackie's walk took her far from the ranch house. When she reached a long-grass meadow, she finally turned back. Picking up a willow switch, she brushed her curving sword back and forth over the green path, singing "Mommas Don't Let Your Babies Grow Up To Be Cowboys" in a whispery voice. She came to a wooden gate she didn't remember, but as she latched it behind her, she looked up to check her directions. The North Star was where she expected, so she must be going the right way. She had gone only a few yards when she slowed, sensing . . . she didn't know what.

Suddenly, she heard a stirring behind her and looked back, only to see a great black mass shadowed between earth and sky.

Her breath caught, then escaped on a sibilant whisper, "Max . . ."

Patting her pockets, she realized she had no treats to give him, no bribe sufficient to belay a charge against a stranger's presence in the bull's territory.

He stood between her and the gate, his great horned head lowering steadily. She backed slowly to one side, unbuttoning her blouse and slipping it off her shoulders. Holding the white material out to her right, she thought she might be able to make the fence before she was gored or trampled.

She felt it before she saw it. Max charged.

Jackie stood frozen, letting her blouse flutter in the breeze. Playing matador, she waited until the last possible moment before she whirled left. He was so huge! His horns tore the blouse from her fingers like tissue paper.

She panicked and ran, her heart ringing in her ears like the bells of St. Mary's. Her breath burned her lungs, and she could feel the thundering of the earth beneath her even as she heard Max's panting breath.

Seeing movement ahead of her, she looked up and saw a horse and rider soar high over the fence, landing to her right. A rope whipped the air, and hoarse shouts sounded. Gray lashed at Max's wide head, no time to make a lariat, no time for better distraction.

Finally, he diverted the bull's attention to himself. Then began a teasing dance, with Gray forcing his stallion Poco to tempt Max closer, only to dart away. Clumps of grass flew through the air, cut by sharp hooves. From the corner of his eyes, Gray saw that Jackie was safe, and he finally let Poco have his head and leap back over the fence. Max slowed at the fence, gave a loud snort and furious shake of his long horns, then trotted away, placid again.

It was Gray who couldn't lose his anger.

He flew out of the saddle before Poco had even come to a halt. Jackie was watching him with her arms wrapped protectively round her body. As if she were outside herself, she watched him grab her trembling shoulders and yank her against his own body.

"Dammit!" he growled into her hair, breathing heavily. "How could you be so stupid?"

"Wh-what?" she stammered. "There was no sign, nothing to indicate Max was behind th-that gate." She was cold, and he was burning hot.

He cursed again, his arms tightening. "Not that. How could you wave that shirt at him, taunting him that way?"

She frowned and tried to withdraw from his arms. He wouldn't release her, and finally she wrenched herself out of his grip, stumbling back a few feet. "My God, do you think I was playing with that animal?"

He looked down at the transparent white lace of her lingerie and forgot what he was going to say. Raising one hand, he jerked at the snaps of his own blue shirt, then pulled it free of his jeans and tossed it to her. He stamped back to Poco and swung up into the saddle.

"Well, come on!" He held out a hand and waited for her to mount behind him.

She turned her back and took her time sliding into his shirt and doing up the buttons. Walking over to the horse, she took his hand and stepped up on his foot to swing behind him. Her arms settled around his waist, and she grabbed tight as he turned a quick full circle.

She made a face at his back. She was on to his cowboy tricks, but it hardly seemed worth calling that to his attention.

A few minutes later the ranch came into view. Gray rode right up to the porch of the main house and slid a hand back to help her dismount. That impartial hand covered a good portion of her thigh and bottom as she slid to the porch.

"Stay out of Max's pasture," was all he said,

though. Then he spurred Poco and rode to the barn.

Jackie mouthed his words mockingly at his back. When he was far enough away, she raised a shoulder to her face and breathed in his scent.

The following week Gray was in Houston on business for three days.

He thought of Jack a hundred times while he was gone, the changes in her, in him, and wondered if she'd even be there when he got back. She still made his body crazy. He couldn't look at her without getting hard. He thought he might very well be falling in love with her all over again. She was different in some ways, though. She wasn't his scared little rabbit anymore, so vulnerable and anxious to please. He'd liked that soft little rabbit, but now she had a confidence and an easy sense of humor that were irresistible.

Three days and he could barely control his impatience to see her. But he had responsibilities, and things were so backed up at the ranch that the afternoon he returned, he immediately climbed into the saddle with a raw bronc. And he banged his knee again.

Then he had to drive out to Harley's to settle a deal they'd made about having his stallion, Wellington, cover a few of Harley's mares.

By the time he parked his truck alongside the barn, he felt ready to be laid out.

Restless and edgy from not having seen Gray for three days, Jackie had decided to make a late night visit to Lucy before turning in. There were only a few aisle lights on in the barn. She found Lucy already half-asleep by the time she arrived.

Pulling the apple from her pocket, she murmured to the mare and held the fruit out for inspection.

Lucy blew out and lifted her lip with great delicacy before her teeth closed over the apple. Jackie laughed softly and let her fingers caress the strong, curved neck and pale mane. Here was warmth, understanding, and there was no betrayal in animals.

She checked Lucy's hay and water, gave the mare a last pat, and eased out of the stall. Glancing to the back of the barn she saw the light on in the tack room. It wouldn't hurt to check, she thought. As she drew closer she heard Gray's voice, mumbling something.

"Graham?" She reached the doorway and gave a start of surprise at what she found.

He sat on the wooden bench under the bridles with his jeans lying next to him. He wore a T-shirt and white briefs, but her gaze fell upon the bright purple bruising around his right knee. He framed the knee with both hands. Beside him lay a small case with a syringe and a bottle.

"Oh, Junior." She stepped into the room. "That looks awful."

"Jack?" His eyes seemed dazed. "What are you doing out here?"

"Just checking on Lucy." She knelt before him. "Are you all right? Should I get Merle?"

Her voice was so gentle, so warm, and he knew she had no idea how it affected him. Its sweetness cut through his pain, and he actually, smiled.

"Lord no," he said, his voice strained, "anything but that. I just racked it up a little. She'd have me in bed for a week, and I've got work to do."

"Maybe that's not such a bad idea," Jackie said dryly, looking closer at his puffy, battered knee. A scar slashed over the top. Her hand came up to touch it before she realized that would only give him more pain. She started to raise her gaze to his, but it caught at the white briefs. She looked away guiltily.

For crying out loud, she thought. Here he was, hurt, in pain, and she couldn't keep her eyes away . . .

"Bad knee," he mumbled, "but it'll be better by morning."

"I heard you quit the circuit because of an injury. This it?"

"Yeah."

"That's for the pain?" She glanced at the silver-topped bottle in the case.

He shook his head. "Swelling."

"Are you taking something for the pain?"

He looked up. There was that voice again, the one that sounded like warm honey. She was so pretty, kneeling there, her eyes full of concern, her blond hair hanging over one shoulder.

He reached out to touch it, catching a strand in his fingers. "I love your hair."

That startled her, he could tell, but she recovered fast.

"You *are* taking something for the pain."

He shook his head and let the golden strand slip away. "But I will if you get the bottle out of that cabinet up there."

Jackie stood and went to the cabinet. When she opened it, she didn't find medication. There was only liniment and a bottle of tequila.

She turned back to him. "No glasses."

He smiled. "No need."

"Ah." She smiled in return and gave him the bottle. "He's such a rugged guy."

He took a long pull, held his breath, and waited for the effect. Then he held out the bottle to her.

Looking as if he'd just challenged her, she took it and drank. He watched her tongue dart out to touch her bottom lip, and sighed in wry defeat.

"One more and you can help me with this," he said. She gave him back the bottle and sent a wary glance at the needle. "You ever learn how to use one of these?" he asked before he drank again. She shook her head.

"Shoot. Guess I'll have to do it myself." He stuck the needle into the bottle and pulled back the plunger. Taking a look at Jackie's face, he added, "You can close your eyes if you want. I won't tell anybody."

"No," she said. "If you can stick that thing into your own leg, I guess I can watch it." She knelt beside him again and put her hand on his other knee. "But if you wait much longer, I'll change my mind."

He laughed and finished readying the needle, then put it in, right behind the kneecap. Jackie was squeezing his sound leg, unconsciously pressing her breast against him. At the last instant her eyes closed, but she opened them when he touched her chin.

"Hey. You okay, babe?"

Jackie swallowed and looked up into his beautiful eyes. They were so light against his tanned skin. "Don't like needles." But she knew he knew that.

She felt the heat of his leg against her, the prickles of the fine hair that grew there. Her gaze fell to the strong line of his thighs and followed to his groin. The soft cotton of his briefs outlined his arousal in perfect detail.

Her breath stopped and her gaze lifted higher, to his lean, powerful chest and arms, his broad shoulders.

It had been so long.

He looked so much a man, strong and sure, and she could see a bit of the coarse reddish hair at the top of his T-shirt that matched the softer hair covering his legs and arms. Still higher was his firm chin, the tender-looking mouth.

Her eyes met his. She wanted to swallow, but couldn't.

He leaned forward, and she knew he was going to kiss her. She didn't feel ready, but she knew it was going to happen anyway.

His lips were as warm, as tender as they looked, as tender as she remembered. They touched hers softly at first, exploring. The next touch was firmer, sweeter. Then he was pulling her up to him, dragging her against his body, and the kiss took on the wildness that was always waiting between them.

With the first touch of his tongue to hers, her mind blanked and dizzied. It was wonderful, better than memory. She was flooded with feeling, and she arched against him, wanting, needing to give back. His tongue explored her, and she let hers entwine with it. She could hear the rasping sound of their breathing, and her fingers were caught in his soft hair as his were in hers.

She could feel every inch of him against her, even that intimate pulse against her belly, and she wanted to cry out at the images that flooded her mind. Suddenly she had to drag her mouth away for air, but he only followed, pressing hot, moist kisses down the sensitive curve of her throat, until he felt her shudder against him. Then his hands were at her waist, smoothing restlessly over her ribs and up to her breasts.

He had such big hands. Ah, but they were gentle as he kneaded her, testing her softness. When he found her tightened nipples, he caught them between his fingers and squeezed as she moaned. She pressed closer, running her own hands over his chest and shoulders, her lips finding his ear.

He groaned in answer and twisted to lift her onto his good leg, but the motion sent a shooting bolt of pain through his bruised knee. He groaned again, this time without pleasure.

"Junior?" Jackie asked softly, sensing the change in his stiffened body. She pulled back. "What's the matter with me? I'm crazy. You're hurt—"

Two fingers pressed lightly against her lips, and she had to stop herself from kissing them.

"Hush, honey." He smiled. "I wanted it, more than you." He warmed again when he saw the blush paint her already pink cheeks. "God, you look beautiful." His fingers traced the line of her cheek and jaw.

"Humph." The sound she made was one of derision. "You don't have to try to flatter me—"

His fingers were back on her lips, then he replaced them with his mouth. "Beautiful," he murmured against her. His tongue touched a corner of her mouth, and she gasped.

"Beautiful," he said again before he put her away from him. "But just now, I think you'd better help me get my pants on."

Six

Jackie was tense and, yes, angry. *Days* had gone by since she had found Gray in the barn, and every hour that passed, she waited for some acknowledgment from him of what had happened. But he said nothing, did nothing.

This time it took longer for him to lose the limp. Every morning he arrived in the kitchen after his brother and Merle. He and Ben talked about the work ahead. Merle would say she was going to make a trip to the grocery or the drugstore or the feed store and did anybody need anything? After breakfast Gray spent a few minutes with Dusty, then the rest of the day working the ranch, coming in to lunch with the other boys.

In the evenings he came to dinner, but again, only after the others were already there. Then he would disappear. She didn't know where he went.

Too many possibilities went through her mind during those days, none of them pleasant. She was certain he'd had second thoughts. Or maybe he was seeing someone else. Maybe he'd only kissed her because he thought she was throwing herself at him.

Well, she could act sophisticated too, and she was tired of the come-here-go-away game.

Gray was just as tense, but for a different reason. Twice he had come close to making love to Jackie. It was a personal thing, but the "stud" of Cross County hadn't been a stud in some time.

He had women friends, but no one he'd let get close since his marriage. During his rodeo years, he'd found the women who came on to him were only after the glamour or his name. He'd been fooled one too many times. After he moved back to the ranch and Tom left, he needed to prove something by sleeping with a lot of women. Maybe prove that he was everything women thought he was. But he only scared himself.

After a series of one-night stands, the idea of finding someone just for sex disgusted him. Yet within hours of seeing Jack again, his whole self had come alive once more. He hadn't really thought it out when he offered her the job. He'd just known that he had to do it. She made him feel more than heat. She made him feel instincts like hunger, tenderness, protectiveness. But those feelings created complications.

If he did sleep with her, Jackie would expect things from him that he wasn't sure he could give after what had passed between them. Intimacy, sharing, love, and dammit, trust! He couldn't give those things, couldn't trust anyone with that much of himself. Not now, maybe never again.

Now that his senses were awake, though, he was having trouble subduing them. As soon as her back was turned, his eyes would be on her. He couldn't stop himself. She thought she wasn't beautiful.

She was to him.

And her warmth, that gentle quality she had, those things were more rare than she knew. Her almond eyes and the scent of her hair haunted him . . . among other things.

Well, he'd started this, and now he wondered just how long he could wait to finish it.

"What's goin' on with you, Gray?" Ben asked him, a concerned look on his face. It was the third time in as many days Gray had made a careless mistake. Once, he'd swung the pitchfork wide and almost impaled Paddy. Later, he'd hammered his thumb and cursed a blue streak. Then he'd walked out of Mercy's stall without thinking to latch it, right in front of his kid brother.

Ben knew something was up.

He looked around to make sure they were alone in the barn before he said anything.

"So tell me. Is the ranch in trouble? Is Dad sicker than they thought? I got a right to know, Gray."

Gray frowned. He had no excuse, at least no good excuse.

"Nothing's wrong, Ben. Pop's fine. Merle's been complainin' too much for him not to be getting better. The ranch, well, you don't have to worry about that." The curly-brimmed hat came off in one hand, and he brushed back his hair with his forearm.

"Oh." Ben's smirk was a knowing one.

Gray stiffened. His little brother looked far too pleased. "Whaddya mean, *Oh*?"

"Well, the only other thing I can think of is woman trouble. And that ain't necessarily a bad thing, considering the woman."

"Get outta my face," Gray said, but Ben only laughed. Gray didn't like being the source of his kid brother's amusement. He'd been the one to educate the kid about men and women in the first place, hadn't he?

"Guess you're about due," Ben said.

"No. I paid those dues."

"Come on, Gray," Ben said, shocked into seriousness by Gray's hard tone. "You can't let your whole life be shoved into a corner because of what you think happened years ago. It makes me nuts when you do that mourning thing. Have you ever even talked to Jackie about it?" He shook his head. "No, you wouldn't talk to Tom about it, either, but you know everything—"

"She left, didn't she, and Tom after her?" The anger Gray felt was explosive. "Well?"

Ben leaned against the stall door. "He'd come back in a minute if you asked him. How long you gonna assume you know everything, Gray? You're so damned stubborn! How long you gonna make the world wait for you to grow up?"

He almost went for the kid. Nobody talked to him like that. Breathing hard, clenching both fists, he struggled for control of his temper. Finally, he managed it.

"You're right, kid." Gray cleared his throat. "Nobody knows everything." He glanced out the barn door. "We got work to do."

Gray held out until Friday night, then he went looking for her. It was nearly eleven when he knocked on her door.

Thinking it was Merle returning her hand lotion, Jackie opened her door wearing only her nightgown. Looking up, and up, she found Gray. One sandy wave of hair fell over his forehead, and his bright eyes had an intent expression.

I can't believe it, Gray thought. She looked like something from his imagination, standing there in a thin cotton gown. It was white, with tiny satin straps and little satin roses across the top. He swallowed hard. He could see the shape of her breasts, even the dark pink color around her nipples. Memory filled out the rest of the picture.

"Junior?" Jackie was too embarrassed to grab her robe, but she couldn't just stand there while he stared at her. She shifted from one foot to the other and ordered herself not to cross her arms. "Is there . . . something you wanted to talk to me about?"

"Uh, yeah." He forced his eyes upward. "Um, what are you doing tomorrow night?"

"Why?" She stood up straight, not realizing that the movement pressed her breasts against her gown.

"I want to . . . uh, take you to a party." He let his gaze flicker down once more before meeting hers.

"No," she said quickly. "Thanks anyway." She started to close her door.

His hand shot out to stop it. "Why not?"

"I . . . don't like parties." She had very vivid images of the kind of people who would be at a party Gray Burton would be invited to at this date and time, and what they would act like if he showed up with his poor ex-wife.

"Then let me take you to dinner," he said. "Maybe there's a movie in town." She couldn't say no, he wouldn't let her.

Jackie was going to ask him why he wanted to take her out. She was going to demand that he explain why he had ignored her. But she looked into his eyes and saw something there that made her whisper, "All right."

"Seven o'clock, then?"

"Okay." She examined her bare toes as a moment passed, full of expectation and uncertainty. She was going to close her door, but had a sudden thought. "I don't want . . . don't make plans for anything too fancy."

"Okay." He would have agreed to anything she asked. "Jack," he said softly. She looked up at him, and he grinned. "Will you wear that tomorrow night?"

She pressed her lips together, but he saw she was trying not to laugh. "Get out of here," she whispered, then she did close the door in his face.

Even after it was closed, Gray stood there remembering the sight of her.

Jackie thought about going into Turbin with Merle to look for a dress, then she cursed herself for feeling the need to impress him. Gray knew what and who she was, and he knew she needed money. He signed the paycheck she got every Friday. Damned if she was going to be so obvious.

Besides, she had a dress that would be fine. It was a sundress, made of a hot pink shine-treated cotton. Though simply cut, it clung to every curve from breast to hip, where it was gathered and flared out to fall below her knees. She had a pair of high-heeled pink sandals, too, though it had been a while since she'd worn anything but flat sandals or sneakers.

She did take the trouble to blow-dry her hair. It took longer than she thought, and there came a knock on her door as she was touching cologne behind an ear.

Looking into the dresser mirror, she took a deep breath and released it. Her eyelashes fluttered nervously as she opened the door.

Gray stood quite still.

This was the girl he'd known so long ago. The pure lines of her face touched him like a healing balm.

"You look . . . wonderful," he murmured.

He hadn't said "beautiful," or "nice," or "pretty." Jackie was glad for that. He had said she looked "wonderful." Wonderful to him.

It must be wonderful indeed.

Or else he'd learned the right words to use on women.

She believed both things at the same time. It was the only safe thing to do and not spoil the dream. And for a while, for tonight, she wanted to live that dream. When it was over, she promised herself, she would put it away and get on with her life.

The hall was softly lit by two wall sconces, and Jackie took a moment to let her gaze drift over the cream-colored gabardine shirt and dark blue jeans he wore, then down to the fancy cobra boots. His sleeves were rolled back, and she had trouble pulling her gaze from the downy-looking reddish hair that ran over his strong forearms.

Raising her eyes to his, she was surprised again at the brightness of them against his deep tan. She could see that the light blue irises were rimmed in a slightly darker color and the gold tips of his feathered lashes fascinated her. His wavy hair was combed and under control, except, of course, for that one place over his right brow.

"Hi," she said.

"Hi, yourself." They'd used the same greeting years ago, and suddenly Gray relaxed. He reached for her hand, and her fingers curled trustingly in his. "Come on," he said, "I'm starved."

She had to skip a couple of times to keep up with him once he started to move. The stairs were a blur, then he was holding open the passenger door of the Lincoln. When he slid behind the wheel, she smelled him and soap and leather, and she wondered at the way his warm presence electrified the air.

Excitement sparkled in her veins in a way she hadn't felt since days long gone. Her hands clasped in her lap, only to fall apart and rearrange themselves on her knees, the seat, and her lap again.

Watching out of the corner of his eye, Gray wanted nothing so much as to pull over and drag her into his arms.

"You said nothing fancy," he said softly. "I hope you won't be disappointed."

She liked him this way, not quite certain of every move he made. Not quite certain of her.

"I won't be disappointed."

He took her to Catfish Sam's. The tables were covered with red-checkered cloths and in the center sat squat, flickering candles.

A small place, with corked nets strung across the wall, they served two things—cornmeal fried catfish and beer batter chicken. Bluegrass music played in the background.

It was early for Saturday night, so there were still a few empty tables. They were led to a dark one in the corner.

"You snake," she said.

"This isn't exactly a metropolitan area, Jack. Besides, Sam's has been here longer than either of us. Now . . ." He turned on the grin that warmed igloos. "Would you like the fine vintage hops or a glass of something akin to Thunderbird?"

"The hops, by all means."

Over beer and catfish she got him to tell her a little about his life in the last few years.

"There's nothing like the feeling of being at the top of the circuit." He looked off into the distance, and she loved the way his eyes sparkled with the memory. "The money was finally great. But I spent it like water. And being in the press and all that attention isn't as much fun as it's cracked up to be. Somebody's always popping out of nowhere with questions and cameras, making up stories and twistin' your words. Hell, you gotta stop scratchin' and spittin' . . ."

Her laugh was low and husky. Gray had never scratched or spit, but she appreciated the sentiment.

For a second, Gray let the sound slide over him. He didn't think he'd ever heard anyone laugh quite the way Jack did, like it was drawn right from the center of her. "The worst," he went on after a moment, "is that you stop feeling like you can trust anybody. Everybody wants something." He said it with rough hesitation, as if he'd never said such a thing aloud before. Sighing, he leaned an elbow on the table. "There's only so long you can live that kind of life. But till you get injured, you keep trying."

Jackie didn't remember Gray like this, so thoughtful and introspective. She liked this wise version of the man she'd fallen in love with long ago.

"You're happy ranching?" she asked. "You never miss the fast life?"

"I miss the rides, the excitement. But you grow

up. You can't play that game till you're ninety, and now I can't imagine doing anything else but what I'm doing."

"Or anybody doing anything else?"

That brought him down quick. "Jack, I'm sorry about that first day. It was such a shock to see you, and I wasn't . . . um . . . very good at . . ."

"Keep going, Junior." Oh, she was enjoying this.

"I was . . . feeling lousy."

"Um-hmm."

"And maybe I was a little judgmental."

She grinned. "Better and better."

"So, I can be a jerk sometimes. Ranching isn't for everybody."

She reached her right hand across the table. "Congratulations."

Startled, he put his hand on hers. Her smile was gorgeous. Just the way he liked it, a little higher on one side than the other, wide and warm.

"That was a very nice apology," she said.

"So . . . uh, what is it you teach in the big city?"

"Taught," she corrected him. "I was an instructor at the university."

"I remember you saying something about that. I'm impressed, Jack, really." Somehow, the handshake had turned to just holding hands. His thumb stroked back and forth over the tender skin of her knuckles. "What's your field?"

"Contemporary American Lit."

He stared in disbelief. "Come on, for real?"

"Yup," she said in her best cowboy drawl.

"Like Robert Ludlum and Zane Grey?"

"More like Alice Walker and Tom Wolfe."

"Why're you here, Jack? You could teach anywhere." And why had she been pushing beer at the Lone Star?

"You really want to know?"

"Yeah, I want to know."

"Well, there are a lot of reasons." She stiffened and looked away, uncomfortable. She would have pulled her hand from his if he had let her. "An instructor's pay isn't that great and when I came here, I found the ranch was in some trouble."

"I didn't think your place was doing that bad."

"I didn't either. But Dad squeezed everything dry at once, the bank accounts, the mortgage."

"Are their receipts for things? Cars, vacations?"

She shook her head. "I stayed around trying to figure things out. Then I found a letter documenting that Doc Bar had stood at stud for Hollywood Lucy." Gray whistled his appreciation. "Some lines, huh? I figured that's where the money went. So when the university told me they couldn't hold my job if I didn't get right back, I found I didn't really want to go back. Coming home was, oh, I don't know . . . Suddenly I felt like the life I had been living was just one narrow line. I felt buried in university boundaries. Ideas, not action. Like maybe I was standing back too far from things that were more important . . . a kind of life that was more full." She leaned forward and smiled mischievously. "You want to know a secret?"

His hand tightened around hers. "Oh, yeah."

She looked down at his dark hand joined with hers. His was callused on the palm and at every joint. She could see two scratches that were healing across the back, and his thumbnail was bruised. A strong, capable hand. "I always wanted to be a rancher." She didn't look back up. She didn't want to see derision in his eyes, or disbelief. "You know how Dad was, he thought girls couldn't do the work. Or maybe he thought they shouldn't . . . that they were too soft or something. Any other man would have been glad of the help. He thought I should always be baking cookies or making curtains. He was a fifties kind of cowboy who just couldn't get over it."

She laughed, finally looking at him again. "You probably thought I just liked to be your audience to watch you move. Well, that's partly true, but I was really horse crazy. I would never have admitted it to you when I was eighteen—everybody told me it was unfeminine—but I used to sneak out to the barn every chance I got. When I was seven, I was swinging on a cable in the barn and fell. Dad locked me in my room every afternoon for a week. And I got kicked in the head when I was ten." She grinned at the way his eyebrows rose. "Well, I learned how not to pick a hoof! Daddy blew his stack over every little accident. I guess it comes with being an only child. Mom didn't know what to do with me either. I mean, I think she understood, but Dad was always boss. When Mom died, he fired the housekeeper, thinking I wouldn't have time to worry about anything else if I had the whole house to take care of."

"Did it work?" he asked.

"No." She laughed again, then sobered. "But it made me find someone who would let me do what I wanted to do—you." She shook her head, as if pushing away the memory. "And when that didn't last, I wanted to get away from all of it."

She wrinkled her nose. "You were supposed to stop me at the part where the lions and tigers and bears came in."

"I didn't want to stop you. I don't remember you ever talking that much about your childhood."

Her chest expanded with her deep breath, and she felt that strange yielding sensation again.

"Tell me about something," he said, then looked down at the table.

"Ye-es?" she coaxed.

"Who hit you that night at the Lone Star?"

She bit her lip. "I really don't want to answer that question. . . ."

He smiled his dangerous smile, and Jackie forgot to warn herself. "Come on, Jack. You've got nothin' to be embarrassed about."

"Another time?" she pleaded, and smiled when he nodded.

He took her to a bar called Charlie's after that. The band was good and loud, and the dance floor was full. Gray walked her right onto the floor and pulled her tight against him. Her hair flew around her face and settled. Her head nestled against his shoulder as they caught the slow beat.

It seemed to Gray he'd been waiting for hours to get her into his arms. Her hair smelled of spring flowers, and there was a trace of some deeper scent, like perfumed soap, under that.

Jackie snuggled closer. His neck smelled like clean, sun-warmed skin. The texture of it was smooth and inviting. His arms tightened around her, and she felt a burning from her chest to her thighs, at the tips of her fingers and palms. Everywhere they touched.

A strangled gasp escaped her when his knee edged farther between her thighs. For a second she saw herself on his bed again, as she had been the night she'd brought him home. But when she tried to draw back, he bent his head and pulled her tighter.

"Stay." His breath tickled her ear. "Umm, you feel good," he said, and she could feel the vibrations of the words in her own body.

She swallowed hard as he rubbed his rough

cheek against hers and every muscle in his body tightened. They moved from side to side. He whirled her around, and her head fell back.

The song ended, and the band went right into another. It was a song she remembered from a long time ago, with a slamming drum and a heartbeat vocal.

Gray's bright, clear eyes looked into hers with open heat. She traced the creases that fanned out from them and one tiny mark from the chickenpox beside his left brow. His warm hands slid over her back from her waist to her shoulders. Down and then up again as if he couldn't stop.

When the song was over, he drew her hand to his mouth and kissed the inside of her wrist.

The guy made her breath catch. No kidding.

Then he took her out of there. They'd never even had a table.

Pulling her after him, Gray got as far as the car door. He leaned her against it and dragged her against him for a crazed, rough kiss that destroyed any trace of resistance she might have had.

His hand moved to her breast, and Jackie felt a quiver that might have been from him or her. She couldn't tell where it started. Her sigh fanned the air, and he kissed her again.

She wanted to rake her hands down the muscles of his strong back, to tell him how much she needed this, needed him. How she had missed him. But she wouldn't. She wouldn't give him that power over her. She just let her fingers find the back of his neck, where his hair curled softly, and she held on.

The kiss became playful. He nipped her bottom lip and down to her chin and back. His right hand gathered the material of her skirt, quickly bunching it higher and higher until he found her stock-inged thigh.

A garter belt . . . he thought. That innocent little dress and underneath, lace garters. "Oh, boy." His eyes squeezed tight as he groaned. His breathing sounded harsh as he slid his middle finger between the top of one stocking and her skin. She shivered. His mouth and tongue played with hers. His finger moved to the inside of her naked thigh, and she bit down hard on his bottom lip.

She jumped back and stared at his chest. Too embarrassed to look at him, she shook her head. "Oh, Junior, I'm sorry," she whispered.

His answer was a low groan as he let his hand slide up to her rounded bottom and pull her hips against him. She felt his body fit hers in a way she couldn't mistake.

She guessed she hadn't hurt him too badly.

His thigh spread her legs, and his hand dipped between them to cup the warmth between her legs.

"Junior," she whispered hoarsely, and he bit her back, on the neck.

If he had tried to take her right there, leaning against the car, she probably would have helped him.

He didn't.

Seven

There was a burst of laughter as a car full of people pulled into the lot, stopping just a few feet from them. Still panting, Gray froze. His hands dropped away, then came up to brace himself against the car on either side of her, blocking Jackie from the light. His head turned toward the noise.

Jackie looked down, hoping they would pass quickly. But amidst the chatter she heard a voice she recognized. It was older, deeper, but Jackie knew to whom that voice belonged.

Sarah Jane Norman.

Sarah Jane, who'd been an expert barrel rider when Jackie's father wouldn't even let her try; who'd had everything she ever wanted; who'd gone away to Smith College in the East. She'd even moved to New York City to model for a few years before she came home.

Jackie peeked over Gray's shoulder and saw three others with her; another woman and two men. She recognized one of the men from her days at the Lone Star.

Sarah Jane had changed her hair color since high school. Hair that had been light brown was now filled with hundreds of blond streaks and cut so that it swung free above her shoulders.

Jackie didn't think Gray and Sarah Jane had gone out in high school, but they had been in the same circle. And Jackie knew Sarah Jane had always wanted him. She might have had him since.

It was at the tail end of a long, trilling laugh that Sarah Jane noticed Gray Burton standing against the Lincoln. She may have dropped "Jane" from her name ten years earlier, but she never forgot the ones that got away. Sarah grabbed Angela and dragged her along for ballast.

"Gray Burton, I haven't seen you in too damn long!" She pulled her girlfriend forward. "You remember Angela, don't you?"

Sarah Jane had to be about thirty now, Jackie thought, but she still dressed like a fifteen-year-old. Her leather skirt barely covered the tops of her thighs, and her friend Angela wore the same outfit in a different color. Both pairs of lips gleamed shiny red.

The sight of that lipstick made Jackie think that, even in this light, she must look like she'd been making out in the parking lot. Her lips were swollen, and her hem was flipped up on one side.

She tried to slap it down without being obvious.

Sarah looked them both over from head to toe. She shook her head at Gray, her smile completely understandable.

"You might introduce us to your friend," Sarah said.

Gray took Jackie's arm and looked down at her, only at her. His dimple showed as he smiled. Sarah Jane was ever obvious, he thought with amusement. "You remember Jackie Stone. Jack, remember Sarah Norman and Angie Bonhomme from Jeff Davis?" He looked up. "And I don't think you've met Dave Bender, Bart Tobb," he added as the two men walked toward them.

"You're Gray's ex?" Sarah said wonderingly, and for the first time, Jackie saw a spontaneous expression cross her perfect face. "I remember you from school. You've changed.

"So!" Sarah turned back to Gray as if she had paid Jackie enough polite attention. "I'm back in town to stay, you know. Daddy's having a barbecue to celebrate, and you'd better come, Gray Burton. It's next Saturday. Oh, you too, honey," she added to Jackie. "It'll be loads of fun. Lots of guys. Oh, Gray, I heard about your daddy. Is he doin' okay?"

Jackie listened to Gray answer and thought, she did that so easily, putting another woman right in place and making her feel like she was starving for a man. Jackie's smile was self-mocking as she decided she hated Sarah Jane.

She watched Sarah Jane and her friend flirt with Gray while his hand played up and down her arm. They looked at him like they'd found the best bite on the plate. Like she wasn't even there to take offense.

Suddenly, she had a blinding flash of realization. Gray was showing her off! He'd danced intimately with her in a public place, then made out in the parking lot! For a second, anger nearly blinded her. Then Sarah Jane and her friends were gone.

Mechanically, she let Gray open the door and put her in the car, but inside she felt raw and hollow.

It was a cold trip back to the ranch. Gray spent

the twenty miles wondering what the hell he had done, going over the things they had said to each other. But the words were innocent, and it would have taken a mystic to catch the undercurrents.

He knew he shouldn't have let things go so far in the parking lot. But he couldn't keep his hands off her anymore. It was just like when they were kids, and there was a kind of joy in that.

Even now, when the woman had herself glued to the passenger door in frozen silence, he wanted to haul her against him. Lord, she was so soft and responsive, flowing right into him.

His hands gripped the wheel, and he shifted in his seat. Things had gone great until Sarah and her friends had shown up.

Was Jackie mad because he couldn't wait to get her into the car before he grabbed her? Did women worry about looking cheap anymore? Nah. That was stupid. Jackie had never been like that, and she had trembled in his arms. He knew she wanted him.

But what now? She was pressing so hard into the door, it looked painful, and he didn't know what to say to her to make whatever it was better.

"I'm sorry, Jack," he started, hoping a blanket apology would at least start conversation between them. But she didn't even look in his direction.

"Me too." The ice was in her voice as well as the air between them.

Sounded pretty final.

He set his mouth and decided to give her until they got back home to cool off. As soon as he stopped in front of the house, though, she was out of the car before he could even put it in park.

"Jack," he called after her. "Jack!"

Jackie turned, reluctantly, from the front steps to watch him walk around the car.

"Why are you so upset?" He looked bewildered and that just made her feel worse.

"I'm not upset," she said in a voice that had no tone. "I'm sorry, Graham. I'm just tired." She tried to smile, then gave it up. "Thanks for dinner. It was very nice. G'night." She turned and ran up the other two stairs and through the front door, leaving Gray staring after her.

Sunday, a week later, and it was far too quiet. Jackie had to get out of the house.

"Merle," she called from the bottom of the stairs.

"Ah'm comin', sugar." A minute later her head appeared around the corner, a small towel in hand. She came halfway down the stairs. "Whatcha need?"

"Is there a horse I can take for a ride?"

"Why, there are four or five." She gave Jackie a hard look. "Ask Paddy to saddle High Card for you."

"Thanks." Jackie's smile was grateful. "I'll saddle him myself."

High Card was a young black gelding with three white socks and a hunter's gait. She galloped him, racing over the dusty plain to the highest ridge she could find, shaking her hair into the wind. If she'd known the land better, she would have kept on, but it started to get too rocky and she didn't want to risk a fall. When she found the ridge, she pushed the gelding toward it. At the top, she trailed his reins and poured water from her canteen into her palm, rubbing it over his velvety muzzle.

While she lay in the soft grass with her hands beneath her head, she stared through the branches of the only tree on the ridge.

No matter how wonderfully last Saturday night had started, it had ended in disaster. And it served her right. Dreams should stay dreams. Hadn't she learned that at eighteen?

Gray followed Jackie's tracks up from the arroyo and found her sleeping under a tree on the ridge.

Leaving his horse with hers, he walked over to her, willing her to wake before he got there. She slept on, one palm pillowing her cheek while the other was stretched out in abandon.

He scraped in a breath and released it slowly before he sat on his heels near her. Hunger swept through him until it was a hard tremor. She looked so young. It took him a minute to figure out she was still only twenty-five.

She was wearing another one of those Mexican blouses. It was turquoise, bright against the green grass, and it fell off one creamy shoulder.

Her hair looked soft and pale, the ends curling as it lay over her shoulders. Thick honey-tipped lashes lay against cheeks that seemed always to glow with an Irish blush. Her full lips were parted in sleep.

He'd like to have kissed her awake. But, no, he shook himself. He wasn't going to do that.

"Jack."

"Junior?" Her eyelashes fluttered, and he swallowed hard at the sweetness that struck him. After all this time, it was her name for him that came first to her lips. But then she was awake and her next words were, "Oh, no!"

"What do you mean, no?" He frowned and bent forward on his good knee.

"I mean go away." She sat up and pushed her hair out of her face, scrubbing the sleep away.

"What?"

"Go! Get away from me. I can't talk to you now."

"I don't understand you!" The anger came swiftly, explosive and full-bodied.

"I know!"

"Well, explain it to me! Tell me what's happening here."

"Either you get it or you don't, Junior. I can't make you understand."

"Well, try, dammit!"

Next thing she knew he was standing over her with his legs wide apart, his hands on his hips.

"Tell me what's going on!" he demanded. "Far as I know, things are going fine between us. You want me. I want you. Hell, they're so fine, we're about to do it standing against the damn car!" *That* made her mad, he could tell. But he was so mad himself, he didn't care.

"You would use that against me," she said fiercely.

"What the hell are you talking about? I liked *that*—in case you couldn't tell—and you! Even though you *can't* speak English! So try, will you? Try to make me understand what went wrong. You've been givin' me the business for a week now. Was it Sarah? It can't be Sarah Norman."

She only looked at him, her eyes wide. When she finally did speak, it was in a whisper and the words spilled out all together.

"What-do-you-want-from-me?"

He looked away, uncomfortable. "I'm . . . not sure I know."

"Maybe I know." Her voice was low with outrage. "Maybe I figured it out."

The tension in the air waved between them like heat signs.

"What the hell are you talking about?" he asked.

"Revenge," she spat out. Her eyes narrowed as she saw acknowledgment flicker across his face. "You were going to show yourself and everybody else how you got me back in the end, weren't you, Graham?"

"It isn't like that, Jack."

"Oh, yeah? You ignored me for days and then suddenly had to have me so much you nearly take me on a dance floor in a bar, then again in a public parking lot?" She snorted at her own stupidity. If he wanted her to feel humiliated, he had certainly succeeded.

"Yeah." He sighed. "I guess I did."

She counted to seven and clawed the grass. "Well, that's nice, Graham. That's real nice that you wanted me." She stared right at him with a menacing intensity. "But what, *exactly*, is that supposed to mean? And what," she went on before he could, "am I supposed to do about it?"

Gray looked up at the wide, cloudless sky. It was beautiful country, and the sky was endless. He grinned his best dimpled grin and laughed, shaking his head.

Yup. This relationship was never going to be anything but crazy. And suddenly he realized that whether he was ready or not, it *was* a relationship. Or it would be if she would just let it.

Tilting his head down, he considered her. He considered the way she tried to look relaxed when she was stiff as a board. He considered trying to talk to her while her fists were held in those tight circles.

He knew better.

So, he bent his considerations and dropped to the ground to lie on top of her. She immediately began struggling to get away, but he pressed harder until she lay still. Then he grabbed her hands in one of his and held them above her head.

"Maybe I don't know what it means," he said. "But I do know that what you're supposed to do"—he threaded the fingers of his other hand though her hair, holding her head still—"is cooperate!" He had to kiss her mad little mouth.

She made an angry noise against his lips and tried to buck him off, but he wouldn't stop. Then she made a funny noise he remembered, a noise he liked. It was pleasure and need. It was surrender.

He was desperate to grind his mouth against hers. Instead, he made his kisses soft . . . and slow . . . and killing. She sighed. Her mouth opened, and he filled it with his tongue, tasting, stroking, taking her own into his mouth and sucking on it so that she would make that soft, helpless sound again.

She did.

Lord, he was hard, and hurting, and loving the anguish of it. This woman did things to him he couldn't believe, things no other woman had. A shudder of emotion quivered through him, and he felt heat rise from his chest to his face. He rocked his body against hers, rubbing the front of his jeans against the heat where her thighs met, needing that friction to stay alive, already imagining what it would be like to bury himself again in her softness.

More, he needed more.

His mouth still joined to hers, he rolled them over so that she lay above him. He let her hands go and pulled down the elastic neckline of her blouse in one motion. As their kiss grew more frantic, he tore open his own shirt and grunted his satisfaction as he felt the contact of flesh to flesh.

They both breathed in gasps.

Her breasts were fuller, more rounded than they had been at eighteen, but sweet with rose tips, already taut.

He gripped her waist, holding down the elastic that pressed her arms to her sides, and lifted her to rub those naked breasts against his hair-covered chest. His own nipples were tight and hard too.

Jackie felt her skin burn and her breath catch. She felt dizzy, her limbs liquid as she drew in his dark scent.

The kiss went on and on as he moved her exactly the way he wanted. It was good, *so good.* They explored with every angle, their tongues finding teeth and cheek, each tantalizing texture. Then his palms covered her, a breast in each hand, her nipples caught between his fingers, making her arch and murmur into his mouth.

That wasn't enough for him either. With a sound of impatience, he stopped that endless kiss and lifted her so that he could catch one of her hard pink nipples with his mouth and draw on it until she bent her cheek to the top of his head. She buried her hands in his feather-soft hair to hold him.

"Jack. Oh, baby. I need you," he whispered, his lips brushing the sensitive skin of her breast with every word. "Tell me you want me too." His voice vibrated through her. "Tell me."

You scare me, she told him silently. *You scare me witless, Junior. And I don't like being scared again.*

"Yes," she said hesitantly, eyes tearing as she

wrapped her arms around his neck and found his lips. "You know . . ." She was aching, empty without him, and she no longer cared whether it was stupid or dangerous or anything.

Her legs straddled him. He cupped her bottom and squeezed rhythmically as he pressed upward.

Her loins felt heavy, and she wanted more than pressure.

Grasping her knees, he lifted her legs over his and rolled her again in one smooth motion. His breathing ragged, his legs braced on either side of her, he sat up. His heart soared at the dazed expression on her face, the naked hunger.

He wanted to tell her how very lovely she was, how much he liked the way she was with Merle and Dusty and the boys, how he liked the way she talked to Lucy and laughed at Ben's jokes. But he wanted this more. He couldn't take the chance, now, that talk would stop it.

Without taking his eyes from hers, he dragged the hem of her blouse from the waistband of her jeans and drew it up, over her breasts that trembled with every breath, over the white shoulders and her thick mane of hair. Then he threw it behind him, his eyes still on hers.

With slow deliberation, he slipped his fingers inside her jeans, behind the snap, and brushed his knuckles back and forth. The muscles in her stomach tightened, and he flicked the snap open with his thumb. The sound of it was loud and crisp.

Pushing with his thumb, he dragged at the zipper, lowering it, his fingers still inside her jeans. Jackie closed her eyes and swallowed. Her bones had weakened, and all of her senses were concentrated on the possibilities of where he would touch her next, what he would do.

Gray's eyes widened. She wore pale peach lace panties. He could even see a little satin bow in the front. She'd always liked fancy lingerie. With one finger, he delicately traced the flowery pattern until it disappeared under the denim.

Jackie's eyes flew open when she felt him nudging her hips, pushing down her jeans, the peach lace going with them. He had forgotten to take off her boots, and her jeans bunched around her feet until he got down there and slipped them away, one after the other. Her socks followed, and he threw everything behind him with an impatience she knew he held in check every time he touched her.

She suddenly became conscious that she was lying on the grass in broad, bright daylight. The sun played through the tree branches and heated her skin. The air smelled of earth and green grass—and Gray.

She swallowed hard again. But then Gray was coming down to her, and he was bare naked, and so strong and beautiful, she wished she could suspend the moment into the years of her life.

An athlete's body, his chest was broad and well-defined, his stomach hard with ridges. His body was fuller than years before, stronger. But he was still darkly tan, with skin so sleek, her fingers ached to touch it and see if it matched her memory.

A masculine triangle of reddish hair spread over the front of him, running a point through his navel and down. The tan stopped at his hips. His arousal rose strongly between them, and her mouth went dry at the sight of it. His legs were long and straight, one knee scarred, each muscle pronounced as he came toward her.

Gray was certain he could feel his blood racing,

heating, pooling in his groin. He was burning up. Falling to his knees before her, he let his gaze travel slowly over her, up from the delicate bones and translucent flesh of her ankles, her knees, over her rounded thighs to the curling blond triangle of hair, her hips and slender waist. He stopped at her breasts, admiring the way the dappled sun splashed over them.

Then he let his gaze rise to her slender neck and over each feature of her face to her brilliant hair. His eyes found hers, and he stared intently, willing her to need this as much as he.

She gave a throaty, pleading cry, and he was there, kissing her, showing his desire with his tender mouth and stroking hands.

He drugged her with kisses that were hot and dark. His mouth was heated, fierce, knowing, and his tongue explored every corner of her mouth until she made a hoarse sound in the back of her throat. Then his lips trailed their magic over her cheek, her jaw, her neck.

His callused fingers slid down her belly to the crisp golden curls. She gasped and waited.

His fingers slipped between her thighs and higher, over her hot, slick flesh, circling, causing every muscle in her body to tighten and quiver and her legs to open to him. He made her tremble and ache. He made her hunger and cry out to him.

Her own hands were no longer idle. At first they touched him in soft, fluttering ways, unsure. They still sent chills. Then she touched him with bold, warming caresses that brought harsh-sounding groans from deep within him.

When she reached between them, he groaned again and put his own hand over hers as she found the velvety skin and caressed him.

For a moment he remembered her threatening

to tell the world about his "overexcitement" problem, and he half worried that he might prove those words. Just to be on the safe side, he lifted her hand to his mouth and touched its center with his burning tongue.

Her gold eyes stared up at him until he kissed each eyelid, her nose, her cheeks. Then, looking into her eyes, he came deep inside her softness.

They both sighed at the moment of penetration, as they had countless times before.

She was tight around him, hot and wet and giving.

"Jack," he whispered. "Ah, baby." The poignant sound of his voice made her want to sob aloud.

It had been a long time for her, and she felt more than pleasure in the burning tightness of his entry. Gray was not small. But with his first flexing move, she began to relax, bit by bit. She could sense his very shape as he came farther inside her, and the pressure became sustaining, not threatening.

When she felt hunger again, and a wild anxiety to be closer and closer still, to take him as far inside her as he would go, her legs wrapped around his hips of their own accord, pulling him deeper.

His hand slipped between them and found the delicate flesh above his entry. Her heart slammed once, then pounded even harder. She wasn't prepared for the ecstasy of it. The layers of sensation bombarding her had taken over, and she was left with nothing but reflex.

Dreamlike, everything had come to slow motion. He stared down at her as if he needed to see all that she was feeling reflected in her eyes.

He moved faster. She gave herself up to his direction.

His back was slick, the skin burning under her fingers. He groaned, pulled her up, and bent to take her nipple in his mouth, tugging until she arched into him.

Her nipple slipped free, and he let her sink down again, his hands teasing the soft skin behind her knees and up to the inside of her thighs. He moved his hips, filling her, pressing against her womb, and she held her breath until she had to let it come rushing out all at once.

"More . . . Give me more."

He smiled a knowing smile and withdrew, then entered again, just a bit, so slowly that she wanted to scream. Her teeth bit into her lower lip as she arched her hips and tightened her legs around him, trying to pull him deeper. "No," she cried, agonized, desperate for release.

He laughed and leaned forward, touching the side of her nose with his in a tender, butterfly caress. He nodded solemnly, his breathing ragged, sweat trailing at his temples. Then he cupped her bottom and drove into her again and again, slow and deep, then faster, wilder, finally hurling her into a convulsive, shattering climax. His own followed, punctuated with a guttural cry.

Eight

They lay side by side, limbs sprawled, fingers almost touching, under the speckled shade of the sycamore tree. Neither wanted to be the first to speak.

Jackie felt as though she had splintered into tiny bits. Chemistry, she thought. It had to be chemistry. That was what her instincts had always told her about this man. That was why she was drawn to him so crazily.

It had been so incredible, so fast and furious. There was nothing calculated or manipulating in what passed between them. She had seen that in his face, the wondering anguish. That had been as exciting to her as each caress. But what did she know? He might look like that, so vulnerable and dear, when he made love to any woman.

Oh, God, this must be what obsession felt like, this not caring about anything, this feeling of "having to have"! Her body had never reacted like that to a look, a touch, from anyone else. She never felt out of control except with him.

She had craved him at eighteen with a fever of

wanting. This was more. His touch made her greedy for all of him. She was a fool to have acted that way with a man who had hurt her so, a man she hardly knew after all these years.

Gray, on the other hand, had probably had too many women to remember the exact number. He had been a professional athlete, in tune with the pleasure and pain his body could give. An athlete in bed, too, he had needed her so often it had shocked her at first. And pleased her.

But now, "incidents" like this must happen to him twice a week.

Gray's breathing calmed, and he turned to her at last, bracing his weight on an elbow. That was when he realized that her eyes were shut tight.

What could he say to her?

He knew he had rushed her. Lord, he couldn't stop rushing her. He always had. But how could he be sorry? Then he realized he hadn't used any protection. He squeezed his eyes shut, visualizing Jackie swollen with his child. She'd been pregnant once before.

Would she hate him? He'd practically attacked her, then neglected to use even the simplest birth control.

Her face was flushed, like a lively, vivid painting. He could still feel the way she had arched into him, so open and needing. The thought of it made him feel as though he wanted to protect her, from anything, everything. It also made him want her again.

He waited, but when she still ignored him, he found a spot where her breast just began to round and placed a tender kiss there. Her eyes opened, and one knee rose in a reflex gesture of defense.

She looked at him and saw his eyes were full of gentleness. His brow and chest were damp with sweat. It made the red-gold hairs darken and turn to tiny arcs.

"You okay, purty girl?" he asked in his morning voice, as he brushed his knuckles up and down the soft skin of her upper arm.

She felt strangely close to tears at his concern, and simply nodded. Maybe he had felt what she did after all.

"You ever gonna talk to me, babe?" He bent his chin and looked up at her boyishly.

That made her laugh slightly, then she shook her head.

"Well," he said, "it's not how I would have chosen it to happen, but I'm not sorry it happened." His look became grave. "Ah, Jack. I've been trying to keep my hands off you since the first minute I saw that yeller hair and those golden cat eyes again." He grinned crookedly. "Seems like the madder you get, the more I got to have you."

Because she wanted to cry so very badly, she took it out on him. "Very funny, Graham." She sat up with unaccustomed awkwardness, then sighed. "But where do we go from here, you and I?"

"Where do you want to go?" His fingers brushed lazily over the side of her hip, then he stopped abruptly and sat up, looking over the rise. He pushed her down again.

"Comp'ny."

"What?" She jackknifed halfway back up.

"Down!" He leaned his body over hers and laughed. "My kid brother would give up chocolate for the rest of his natural life if he could find me in a 'compromising position.'"

He wasn't expecting her to toss him off with such strength, and he rolled over twice before he stopped. Jackie poked her head over the rise and saw that Ben was, indeed, riding in their direction. Bent over nearly double, she scrambled to where Gray had thrown her clothes and got into them as fast as she could.

"He won't see us if we're just careful not to stand," Gray said calmly. Watching her, he wondered if she had been caught before to cause such haste.

"I don't want to be careful," she snapped as she dragged up her jeans. "I don't want to have to be *careful* any more than I want to be shown off like a trophy!"

By the time she tucked in her blouse, Gray had pulled on his own jeans. The fly was still wide open as he came toward her, just near enough to be out of his brother's sight.

"I've seen you do this before, Jack. Don't."

"Don't what?" she asked while she tugged on her boots, as if the answer couldn't possibly matter to her.

"Since you came back to town, I've seen how— Whenever I get too close, you find something to be mad at me about, some way to stop it. But I don't believe it's what you really want. I just don't believe it."

Her hair flew through the air as she jerked her head up. "Of course, you've become so practiced at the art of 'have 'em and leave 'em' that you could never say or do the wrong thing at the wrong time, could you?" He tried to speak, but she cut him off. "Maybe you can't order me around anymore, Junior. Maybe I'm a full-grown woman now and you don't know me at all!"

"What are you talking about?" His chin lifted like he'd just taken a hard punch.

"I'm talking about this"—she looked around— "and last Saturday night, and you taking what you want." Her eyes seared him. "Seems pretty clear to me you just don't know how to ask! Well, I'm not the naive, brainless girl you swept off her feet eight years ago. Did you think only the great Graham Burton had the right to walk away first? Well, it was a real good time, Graham. I think you did learn somethin' at the rodeo. But was I supposed to throw myself at your feet and declare my undying love now?"

"Don't do this, Jack."

"I'm not easy anymore, Gray. That girl died in a cow-town motel. You know, I waited at that bus stop for ten hours before I realized you weren't coming for me. I thought you'd come find me and get down on your knees apologizing for ever doubting me. I never thought you'd let me go . . . but you did." She pushed her hair back over one shoulder as he bent his head and rubbed his eyes. "And now I don't fall for cowboys with sweet lies, so maybe you better just stick to your usual and leave the hired help alone. That way you'll be sure of all the rules."

"I never lied to you," he said.

"And I never lied to you," she answered sharply.

His eyes were sad when he looked at her, and angry. But when he turned away, she knew she was safe.

She rode down the other side of the ridge and, though she had thought to avoid him, ran into Ben. She couldn't know how full of turmoil her face was, or how the whisker burns showed against her delicate skin.

"Hey, Jackie! Got some sun, huh?" Ben said as he looked over the next ridge for strays.

"Hmm." She unconsciously imitated his brother, and Ben turned away to hide his grin.

"There's my date." He pointed the brim of his

hat at a cow stuck in a muddy ravine about twenty feet away. He put his heels into his mare's side and took the rope from its place against his saddle. "Wanna help?" he called back.

"I could be bribed."

They got home late in the afternoon, covered with mud, both of them exhausted. The cow, whom they'd dubbed Cruella after the first few minutes, had buried herself in mud up to the shoulders. After a half hour of pulling from two directions, Jackie got down into the mud with her.

Ben wanted to do it, but they needed the stronger of them up on dry land, doing the pulling part with both horses while she pushed. And the fact that he made no bones about asking made Jackie heartily grateful.

She came away with two broken nails, strained muscles, and an unspecified number of bruises.

She had the time of her life.

They stomped onto the porch and shed their boots, laughing and taking turns naming Cruella's future offspring. The bull calves would be Chainsaw and Sadaam, the cows Orca and Bliss.

"Bliss?" Ben squinted as he hopped on one foot and tugged at a boot.

"Yup." Jackie scratched her cheek, leaving a dirty streak behind. "Let somebody else learn through experience."

That set them off again until they remembered that they would have to take turns with the hot water. This realization started a mad dash through a field of countless obstacles, including Gray and Merle, to the stairs and up. Jackie's bathroom was closer, and she made it first, squealing in triumph.

Ben laughed. "Okay, I give. It was worth it to hear you squawk like a chicken."

She threw a towel at his head. It made a perfect

tent over him. "Sore loser." A giggle escaped, and she jumped inside the bathroom, locking the door before he could retaliate.

She turned on the water and dropped her clothes to the carpet. Finding her bath crystals, she poured them in until their scent overpowered the smells of mud and sweat. But above the aches Cruella had caused, her body still hummed with the sensations aroused by Graham Burton, Jr.

Gray waited through an endless dinner, marked only by his brother's enthusiastic account of the dramatic rescue of Cruella and Merle's chuckles at the picture they must have made. After dinner, he waited in the barn, puttering around Poco and his other favorites and talking to himself while the stars came out in bright relief.

Finally, he let himself remember what had happened two weeks before his wife's nineteenth birthday.

Gray put his key in the lock and entered the motel room, sighing tiredly. His Stetson sailed through the air to land on the cheap Formica dresser.

"Jack?" he called. "I'm done early, babe."

No answer came back to him. He checked the tiny bathroom. She wasn't there either. Strange, he thought, but she couldn't have gone far. He had the truck.

He squeezed the tight muscles of his neck with one hand and reached for the doorknob with the other. Maybe Tom knew where she was.

A few doors down he started checking numbers. When he found the one he wanted, he gave a cursory knock and turned the knob. As he stepped into his brother's room, he saw Tom, his back to the door, standing hunched over.

"Hey, you seen Jack?" Gray asked. Then he caught sight of the hem of a robe and a pretty pair of bare feet and ankles showing between Tom's legs. He grinned wickedly. "Sorry, guy, I was lookin' for—"

That was as far as he got. Tom had turned awkwardly toward him, and his arms fell away from the woman he'd been embracing. Her face was streaked with tears, and her hair was a mess. Her eyes were filled with pain and something that looked like fear.

His mind went blank as he stared at her standing there in his brother's thin flannel robe. Time wrapped around him in dizzying circles. She had a beautiful body. He could see the shape of her breasts against the material.

Then a rage of betrayal swept through him and he lunged at Tom with a feral growl.

"Gray," Tom said urgently, holding up his arms to fend off his younger brother. "Stop! It's not—"

His words were cut short by the push Gray gave him. Tom went flying across the bed, into the wall, and down to the floor.

Gray never even heard Jackie scream for him to stop, never saw her run out the open door. In his mind he kept seeing the picture the two of them made embracing beside that rumpled bed.

He looked over at the brother he had worshipped most of his life as Tom got to his feet. Fists clenched, he struggled with a fury more potent than he'd ever felt.

"Gray, for God's sake!" Tom cried out.

He looked around. Jackie was gone. He started for the door.

"You idiot!" Tom yelled. "Jackie had a miscarriage, damn you! Her clothes were covered with blood!"

Gray shook his head and gave his brother one last glance. Then he stomped out, slamming the door so hard it crashed twice against the wall before falling off the top hinge to hang there drunkenly.

When he entered their room, she was packing. "Don't say anything," she said quickly, without turning.

"Where do you think you're going?" he demanded.

"I don't know. I just know I can't stay with you." She still didn't look at him.

Leaving him! Why was she leaving him, unless . . . "Was it mine?"

She turned at that, and it all came tumbling out. "I'm going. I can't stand this anymore. I remember when we used to talk, we used to have fun. I never see you, I'm just stuck in one motel room after another. I can't get a job or go to school. You're taking so many chances, Junior, just for the money. And you won't let me be a part of anything. You treat me like some kind of groupie, until you think some cowboy might be coming on to me. I'm more than that!"

"Was it mine?" he asked again. Why didn't she answer him?

She turned back and closed the suitcase, her head shaking ruefully. "You had to ask me that."

His voice became steely. "When did it happen, then, Jack? We've used something from the first time we were ever together. Hell, I've been so afraid to get an eighteen-year-old girl pregnant, I dream about it at night."

She picked up her purse and suitcase. "Don't worry anymore," she whispered.

Panic slammed his chest, making his voice harsh. "You can't just go . . ."

"Don't try to stop me. I'll only wait till you leave for the fairgrounds."

"Then I won't go."

She stood facing him, heartbreak in her eyes. "Don't make it turn to hate, Junior. I can't bear for that to happen."

He reached out to her, finally realizing her pain, needing to comfort her.

"No." *She flinched back, away from him.*

Shock and hurt smashed through him, and he whirled around in frustration. Staring at the cheap print over the bed, he was overwhelmed by a feeling of dread, of disaster. How had this happened to them? When had it all turned so bad?

He heard the door close and started to go after her. Then he stopped himself. Doubt clouded his mind. She wouldn't be leaving him if it had been his baby.

"Was it mine?" *he whispered to the empty room.*

It was after midnight when Gray finally opened Jackie's door. Moonlight poured through the window onto a patch of carpet, and he heard the door latch quietly behind him.

Jackie clicked on the bedside lamp, startled awake by the sound. Gray was still dressed in jeans, but he was barefoot. She watched as he made his way to her bed, wondering why she felt no indignation at the intrusion. The pain was there, but somehow she had known he would come to her like this.

He was a beautiful man, a strong, special man. No, it wasn't indignation that she felt.

"You're awake," he said. "Good."

"What is it?" she asked in a sleepy voice.

Standing by the bed he spoke softly, "It's time we talked. Can I sit down?"

As Jackie moved over, he saw she was wearing a schoolgirl's pink cotton gown with puffy sleeves. His frown was serious as he crossed his arms over his chest and leaned back against the headboard. Though he was careful not to touch her, he felt her warmth across the distance between them.

"I want you to believe what I'm going to say to you now, 'cause it is the God's honest truth." He waited for that to soak in before he continued solemnly, "I was never trying to prove I could have you back. I've said this is the truth, so I'll tell you that the thought might have crossed my mind for a second when I first saw you, when I was still fighting my feelings." He looked straight at her, open and vulnerable. "But I could never deliberately set out to hurt you. I just couldn't, Jack." He sighed. "You were wrong . . . about that."

She stared down at the coverlet.

"Having you in my life again has made me think long and hard about what happened between us." He gave an angry shake of his head. "I look back now and I still don't understand. Six months of wonderful and suddenly, we . . . didn't talk anymore. I panicked. Inside, I knew you would never have slept with Tom or anyone else. But I knew you were unhappy. It was taking too long for me to make money on the circuit. I was crazed with all these emotions I didn't know how to handle; love for you, competition with Tom, insecurity about being a man and taking care of you right. It just all came at me so fast, I couldn't think.

"I need to tell you I'm sorry, honey. I'm sorry I didn't love you better, trust you more. I'm sorry about our baby."

She couldn't speak for a moment. Finally, she whispered, "Nobody could hurt me the way you did."

"I know." He forced the words from his tight throat. "Because I know what I felt like when you left me."

When she sat up to grab a tissue, he spoke again. "I still can't seem to do the right thing around you, Jack. But I can't stop thinking about you, wanting you. I touch you and I don't know where I am. Worse, I don't care."

Jackie swallowed hard. God help her, she understood.

"Do you want to forget what happened today?" he went on.

"Do you?" she asked back.

"No."

She didn't know what she wanted, but she did know one thing she had to say. "I won't be railroaded and I won't be handled."

"I see that," he said earnestly. "Well, you can yell at me anytime if you think that's what I'm doin' to you. And I can try and change how I deal with you, Jack. But I can't change who I am. I've been foreman for a long time now. I'm used to getting my own way."

She gave his big body a sidelong glance and didn't wonder at it. *You always were,* she thought.

"But that doesn't mean I don't respect your right to decide," he continued. "I would have stopped making love to you if you hadn't . . ." He hesitated.

". . . Given in to you?" she finished for him.

"Not to me, Jack, to us. To what happens when we come together. I'll do what I can to show you I value your choice, but I can't control what happens between us. I never could."

He looked down at her bent head, watching as she absorbed his words with a childlike nod. Jackie was thinking that he was right. It was like a fireball of emotion between them, and it seemed neither of them could anticipate its explosions. That almost pleased her. At least it made her feel less alone.

"What else?" he asked.

She took a deep breath. "I won't be lied to," she said carefully.

"Lied to? What are you talking about? I never lied to you!"

"If you're seeing someone, tell me now."

She felt his hand warm on her hair, at the nape of her neck. "No, babe, there's no one else."

He was using that voice on her again, and it was working.

She lifted her head stiffly. "Don't expect me to believe that too easily, old buddy, old pal. Remember me? I was there. I know . . ." She took a breath. ". . . what you need."

"Yeah, well." He laughed gently. "I was twenty-three years old and crazy in love."

"Oh."

A couple of minutes passed.

He looked deep into her eyes, then cupped her face in his big hands. "What I feel with you, woman, I haven't felt . . ." His eyes closed, and her heart rose in her throat. When he looked at her again, he said, "Jack, I wasn't looking for this. Then, there's the fact that everybody knows your business on a ranch. I want to . . . make sure you know what you're letting yourself in for." His hands dropped away, and he raked one through his hair.

"Are you saying . . . ?" She sat up and looked

at him uncertainly. "What are you saying, Junior?"

Gray's eyes mesmerized her. They seemed dark, for once, the purest blue of the deepest sea.

"I want to be with you, if you'll let me, for us to be together as much and as often as possible."

She dropped her head down again. "Why?"

He gently lifted her chin, and she saw surprise in his eyes. "Don't you know?" Now passion flared in his eyes, too, waiting for her. When she blushed and tried to duck her chin, he held tighter and bent to whisper against her lips. "Don't you know how you make me feel, how you make me laugh? Can't you tell how crazy you make me?"

"We're not from the same world, Graham. We never were," she whispered back against his mouth.

That made him laugh and complete the kiss. His beautiful lips were so soft, slanting one way, then the other. When he pulled back, she tried to follow. He pushed her hair behind her ear and chuckled. "Honey, we grew up together in the same little town."

She shook her head in frustration, "Money, Junior," she said meaningfully. "Money."

"Come." He leaned back on the bed and reached for her again. She couldn't help it, she wanted to go back into those hard arms.

As she snuggled against him, he brushed his lips over the top of her head, drawing in the fragrance of her hair. "So, it's not me you object to anymore, just my dough?"

She made a huffy noise and mumbled into his neck, "That's only the most glaring problem."

"Oh, yeah?"

"There are others. Well, look where we are . . ."

"I know, I know . . ." His hands were straying.

"Thirty feet from your father's room."

"Ouch."

"So watch that hand," she instructed primly, though her nerve endings were sizzling.

"I have an excuse."

"Really . . ."

"It's got a mind of its own." He felt the laugh she held back.

She closed her eyes wearily. "You're the last complication I need."

"Ah, but you are just exactly . . . exactly what I need." He leaned down and gave her another one of those perfect kisses. Her heart was wild and her blood burned. His voice fell over her in a steady stream. "We have something most people don't ever have, Jack. I don't care that you're afraid. I don't care that you're workin' here." He tossed his head back arrogantly. "Or that you happen to make all the men who work for me crazy too." He kissed her again, and she sensed a kind of restraint in it. "You can believe this or not, but I'm through ruining my life with jealousy or fear."

"What did you ever fear?" she tossed back.

He snorted. "Everything. Having you, losing you. Fear of making a fool of myself, of losing to another rider. I know what I was, and I know what I am." Gentle, callused fingers curved over her breast in a way that shortened her breath even more, then slid down to cup the curls between her legs. "You don't trust me or anyone. I understand why. But I can't take your money, 'cause you don't have any." He waited for her shocked laugh. "I won't do you wrong." He sent her his most devastating grin. "But go ahead and watch me like a hawk. It's okay by me." He got serious again. "But no more excuses, Jack, no more rules. Come here to me."

He hauled her tighter against him and grinned down at her. "Closer." He growled. "You keep on keepin' watch and let me make some time."

He made her reckless. How was this happening? Jackie wondered. She pulled her mouth from his with an unexpected strength and whispered, "We can't . . . Merle and Ben and Dusty . . ."

"They didn't see me." He drew back enough to look into her green-brown eyes, framing her face between his hands. "Kiss me."

A part of her must have been waiting for permission to do just that, because at his words something in Jackie seemed to come apart and the fire of that damn yearning started again. He kissed a place just behind her ear.

"Come on."

She felt his groan against her throat before he pressed his lips in a slow, heated trail around to her nape.

Devil, she thought. How could he still remember?

His teeth scraped over the sensitive skin, and his arms tightened for a moment, then he tore the covers from her, dragged her up high against his chest, and turned so that she lay on top of him.

She gasped, grabbing for his shoulders.

His mouth found hers with exquisite force, and she moaned as his tongue met hers. His urgency had her trembling, and she arched closer.

"I think I like you at my mercy," he said between kisses. His hot breath teased her ear, and she felt every hard inch of him before his hips lifted against her. He kissed her again until she didn't have a single objection left.

His lips and tongue were weakening her bones.

His body was powerful and gorgeous, and she caressed his chest, tugging at the buttons of his shirt. She wanted the hot feel of his skin.

Groaning, he pulled her hand down and over his hard length, guiding her fingers in the way he wanted her to touch him.

"Ah, babe . . ." His cheeks flushed, and that vulnerable look came over his features. There was something so erotic about that look. Her breath came in short gasps as she continued the sensual motion and felt him grow even larger in her hand.

Suddenly he rolled again, sweeping her beneath him. Elbows straight, he rose above her and looked down into her eyes. He smiled.

She lifted one hand to his jaw and stared back. Slowly, tenderly, he turned his head and rubbed his cheek into her palm. She felt the sandpaper burn of his beard, and her eyes closed languidly. He pulled away, and her eyes flew open in time to see him yank off the rest of his clothes. His body looked immense, tightly muscular, and . . . very ready.

By the time he was beside her again, Jackie was having trouble breathing at all. Her gown had slipped up to her thighs, and when he lay on top of her again, his hands rode the sensitized length of her legs, snagging the thin cotton up over her hips, then over her head.

Impulsively, she reached out with both hands for him. The expression on his face made her glad she had. He overwhelmed her with his heat, the strength of his passion. His kisses were carnal, rough, and explosive. His furry chest teased her breasts, and her legs parted to allow him to settle his hips between them.

His lips found a pink nipple, and she twisted as

he nibbled softly. When he drew on her, tugging with lips and tongue, she sighed, her hips arching upward into the cradle of his. Her hands kneaded the thick muscles of his shoulders and skimmed over his hard arms.

"Oh, yes." His eyes burned her, as did his husky voice. "This feels so good, you feel good." His hands slid beneath her and squeezed before he massaged lightly at the base of her spine. "Softest skin, so white . . ."

A shudder ran through her. "I can't take much more, Junior," she whispered, shaking.

His answer was to dip his tongue into her navel, which sent her hips skyward once more. "Oh, yeah?" He kissed the satiny skin of her belly. His fingers traced the shape of her knees as he put his lips to the hollow spot high inside her thigh.

"Oh, Junior," she murmured.

She shook at the first hot touch of his mouth between her legs. She was beyond embarrassment, beyond self-consciousness. He kissed her deeply, sucking at her flesh, soothing her with his tongue, then biting with his teeth until she moaned.

"Yes, give me . . ." he whispered against her, feeling the tension rise in her body. He took his time, his thumb flicking at her as his tongue plunged deep. With a last convulsive tremor, she sobbed her satisfaction, the back of one hand over her mouth as she stifled her cries. He surged up beside her and took her in his arms to hold her tight. She felt him press hard against her thigh.

"Jack," he said, his voice rough and unsteady. "You don't know what it does to me when you do that."

She turned into him and pressed frantic kisses

across his warm throat. His hips moved against her, and her shaking hand found the taut, velvety skin of his arousal once more. Her mouth brushed downward over the rough curls that covered his torso as her hand moved upon him. She licked at a masculine nipple and felt it tighten under her tongue, felt the tripping of his heart. Then she let her lips follow the hard lines of his muscular chest.

Her mouth burned him, and he cried out in a hoarse voice, far too aroused to maintain any control. Her hand held him steady as she ran kisses around and over, her tongue circling the tip as he bucked beneath her. Finally she pulled him to her, whispering, "I need you . . . inside me—now."

"Wait." He reached for his pants, digging for the foil packet. He stopped and kissed her solemnly, then watched her as he ripped it open. She exhaled slowly. He took her hand and had her help fit the second skin over him. That done, he kissed her mouth, turning this way and that, until she thought of nothing but him.

He filled her slowly, completely, and his eyes didn't leave hers. Never in her life had Jackie felt so close to any human as she felt in those moments, and the pleasure his body gave hers was beyond description.

The heat, the rhythmic thrusting, became the focus of her entire being, and she wanted, needed so much that she felt like screaming her frustration. When his mouth found her breast again, she arched, panting, and was thrown into a diamond blackness of the most exquisite, trembling sensation, only to feel his explosive release follow.

His weight was comforting as he lay slumped on

top of her. After a time he moved to the side without letting her out of his arms.

Whispering her name, he buried his face in her neck, and she reached to pull him closer yet.

Nine

Gray held her all night, waking her to make love again, like stoking a slow fire. Just before the alarm, Jackie woke, quickly for once, shocked to find him still in her bed. He didn't budge as she scooted out from under his arms and the covers.

The night before replayed itself in her head as she readied herself for the day and began breakfast. Her body was sore, but she felt good—very, very good—and charged with a wild happiness and the certainty that her life had changed. She was bent over the open door of the oven when she sensed his presence behind her. She straightened carefully.

His hands encircled her waist and pressed her back against the warm length of him in a hard squeeze.

"I missed you," he murmured into her hair as his hands slipped over her hips, her thighs. A gentle kiss found the side of her neck.

Her movements were jerky as she put the biscuits on top of the stove. "Sit down," she said over the lump in her throat, "and I'll get you some coffee."

Glancing up, she found him watching her with a worried look. She didn't know what caused it, but when she put the cup before him, his fingers brushed hers—and held tight for a minute.

She smiled tentatively and saw the worry change to gladness.

"I made an appointment for Dad's vet to come look at Lucy today," she said when she had the width of the room between them once more. "Will you have somebody call me when he gets here?"

"Hmm."

"And stop looking at me like that," she hissed.

He grinned. "Like what?"

"Like you're about to grab me and throw me across your saddle."

He was still beaming when Ben came rushing into the kitchen. He stopped short at the sight of the two of them looking so . . . smoothed out. He managed not to say anything, just poured his coffee and snatched a biscuit from the stove.

Merle had no such compunctions. She came barreling in, grumbling about how she *had* to have a vacation. As soon as she had coffee in hand, she looked around the room, from Ben to Jackie to Gray. "Well, what's the matter with ever'body?"

Ben sputtered into his coffee, and Jackie burned her finger. Gray cleared his throat.

"Sheeez." She took her seat with her usual aplomb and disregard for distractions. "So, kids, we got a problem." Three pairs of eyes riveted upon her. "Dusty's gettin' restless. He could use some kinda diversion. Ah think Ah might take him up to the lake in a few days."

"Sounds like a good idea," Gray said blandly while Ben grinned.

After lunch, Paddy came to tell Jackie that "the doc" had arrived. Jackie pulled off her apron and followed him to the barn. Still preoccupied with questions she needed to ask, she hardly noticed the woman standing outside talking to Ben. He stared at the woman so adoringly, though, Jackie did a curious double take and saw the big black bag.

Her mouth dropped at the same time her steps faltered. There had to be a mistake, she thought. Her father would never have trusted a woman, not with his horses.

The woman turned. She had long brown hair, streaked with a wing of white, that lay over her shoulders like a curtain. She also had the most gentle face Jackie had ever seen.

"You must be Bill's girl Jackie." She held out a hand, and her grip was all business, cool and firm. "I'm Caro Simpson."

Jackie's smile had to have shown some of what she was feeling, because Caro looked amused and said, "I think I got that very same look from Bill the first time I came to his place on call."

"I'm sorry." Jackie felt like a traitor to her sex, to the fight she had fought most of her life. "It's just that I'm surprised. My father . . . I mean, he wasn't very trusting of women, not for things he thought men should be doing."

Caro laughed. "Don't I know it. But when I arrived he had a mare in labor with a breech. Despite the 'words' we had, I put him to work and he did such a good job we were friends ever after—even when I beat him at poker."

Jackie smiled. "Can't seem to shut my mouth."

Caro lifted both brows and said matter-of-factly, "Happens all the time. So . . . I'm looking for a mare who looks like she's had far too many apples."

Lucy whickered in greeting as they neared her stall, and Caro pulled some sort of oat stick from her pocket. "Can't conscience sugar," she muttered, "so I make these up and bake them with honey." Jackie was then largely ignored as Lucy nodded her head, whickering again while Caro murmured in a soft, musical voice and stroked her neck. Jackie relaxed. These two were obviously quite happy with each other's company.

The vet put her stethoscope to Lucy's belly and hesitated, then touched four more spots.

Caro asked for a sink, and Jackie held the mare's head through the rest of the examination, then led the way back to the tack room.

"Should be about three weeks," Caro said when she had finished at the sink for the second time. "You excited?"

"I thought I hid it so well," Jackie responded. "Everything look okay?"

"I'll tell you, I'm not crazy about the sound of that foal's heart."

Alarm flashed through her, and she stared at the vet.

"It'll probably smooth out as time goes. It's not terribly unusual." Caro gave her that gentle smile. "You have my exchange number. I know this foal meant a lot to your dad." She looked around. "Dusty and his boys keep a good clean barn. Make sure she gets daily exercise, and I'll give you some more vitamin supplement."

"Thanks," Jackie said. "I appreciate it. What should I look for?"

"Changes in food consumption or behavior, but I really don't expect any. I'll go up to bother Dusty a minute, then I'm due at Kelsey's for a seed collection."

Jackie gave a little laugh.

Caro grinned back. "Yeah. Somehow the romance is missing." She strode down the aisle of the barn, then turned, quickly and gracefully. "Jackie?" She looked thoughtful. "You play poker?"

"Yes, indeed." Jackie stuck her hands on her hips. She liked this woman.

Caro nodded her satisfaction. "Good."

As the vet left Jackie buried her anxiety about Lucy deep, as deep as she could.

Over the next few days, she found much to occupy her. She loved it, but caring for Lucy took up a lot of her time. She made a trip to town to go to a doctor of her own, tired of foil packages. Although she soon wondered if she should have bothered. Though she and Gray had sneaked off together a couple more times, he'd suddenly become invisible around the ranch, his jobs taking him away from the house and corral from dawn to supper. Frustrated by his apparent avoidance of her and trying not to imagine the worst, Jackie drove off to her own ranch one afternoon to check on how things were going there.

Rand was a lean, tough, dark-eyed cowboy who looked like he'd been through the cowboy wars. His wife Jenny, on the other hand, was strawberry-blond and baby-faced. She couldn't have been taller than five feet, and her eyes brimmed with mischief.

Jackie had called ahead so that Rand would

have the time to look over the horses with her. Jenny was waiting on the porch.

"Hey!" Jenny called when Jackie drove up. She flew down the plank steps.

Jackie grinned. She had to. That was the effect Jenny had on everyone. "How're you doin', Jenny?"

"Just great! Rand was meant to have a place of his own." She smiled. "I don't think you'll recognize him."

Jackie's eyebrows rose as she took another look at Jenny's pedal pushers and overblouse. "Jen, are you . . . ?"

A soft laugh was her answer. "January."

Jackie smiled. "What do you want, boy or girl?"

"I don't care and I don't want to know, as long as it's healthy and looks like Rand." When Jackie's eyebrow rose higher with her smile, Jenny said definitely, "I want it to look *just* like Rand!"

Jackie let her smile slip. You had to admire the devotion.

Jenny nodded and took Jackie's hand. "Let's find my man. I know he's foolin' with some horse."

Rand was in the third stall, disinfecting a scratch on Bandolino's hindquarters. Their approach was quiet, but he looked behind him on instinct. Even from where they stood, Jackie saw his expression soften at the sight of Jenny. Jackie smiled, touched again.

Jenny had been right too. Rand looked different, his face, his stance. A kind of gentleness had settled around him.

"Hi," she said. "And congratulations."

His answering grin was wide. "Just a minute, Jackie."

"Oh, you don't need to hurry on my account. I

wanna talk to the monsters, let 'em tell me they missed me . . . stuff 'em with carrots."

Rand grinned again. "Bag's in the tack room."

The next night, Merle announced that she and Dusty would be leaving for the lake cabin in the morning.

Gray frowned. "I don't know, Merle. He's still barely getting to the john by himself." His jaw clenched and he shook his head. "He looks so much older than before the accident. Maybe you should wait a week or two."

Merle started to speak when she was interrupted by Dusty himself, leaning on the doorjamb.

"Well, I ain't dead yet," he groused in his smoky voice.

"Pop."

"Dad."

Gray and Ben overlapped as they jumped up to help him. He stared them down with a force that reached across the room.

The awkward moment spilled out until Jackie lifted her knife. "Hiya, Dusty. You still hungry?"

Dusty sat gingerly in his own chair at the head of the table. "I wouldn't mind another piece of that apple pie and a cuppa cof—" Merle had only to make a sort of throaty, humming noise, and Dusty finished with, "that herbie tea."

In silent accord, Gray and Ben worked hard at disguising their expressions while Dusty's leathery visage combined affronted dignity and bulldog determination.

Jackie put her chin in hand. "So, what kinda fish you get up there, Dus'?"

"Fattest catfish you ever saw, little darlin'," he said gleefully. "I'll bring you back a necklace."

"And who's gonna clean 'em?" she asked challengingly.

"My boys," he announced without a qualm, and things were settled.

Later that night Jackie was coming out of the pool house just as Gray was going in. They collided at the doorway. Gray pushed her back inside, his ribs to her chest, and closed the door.

"Finally," he said, satisfied that she was alone.

Jackie was holding her damp suit and had nothing on under her long terry robe. She had planned to go in the patio door and right up to her room after her swim.

"Thanks for what you did at dinner," he said as he knotted his hands behind her neck, under her wet hair. He made every nerve in her body spark to life so easily. She found herself staring, absorbing the look of him, his brilliant eyes, the pleasing turn of his lips. It seemed so long since he had touched her.

"What did I do?" she asked.

"Well, let's see." He kissed the corner of one eye, letting her fluttering lashes tickle him. "You saved me from having to explain to my father that I don't think he's senile." He kissed her nose. She had a beautiful nose, slender and straight. "You saved my father from having to try to beat the . . . to beat his sons to a pulp to prove his strength." His lips found the other brow and brushed lightly. "You helped guarantee that I could find more time to harass you while they're gone—and for that I am truly grateful." His mouth nipped hers, then he looked into her haunting eyes and said quietly,

"I never thought he'd hear me say a dumb-ass thing like that."

Jackie ran a loving hand through his hair. His forehead was bronze against the paler skin of her fingers. "Don't worry."

"Hmm?"

"Don't worry. It's much too small to worry about."

He stared down at her. When he bent his head to kiss her, his hands smoothed over her slender shoulders and down. Jackie felt her muscles tighten, and her suit dropped from nerveless fingers.

His tongue parted her lips and searched her mouth for the sweet, hot desire he always found there.

Jackie felt a tremor shake her, amazed that he could have carried her so far, so fast. She blinked, strangely light-headed.

"No," she whispered, her eyes shut tight.

"Yes." His voice was hoarse, his hot breath caressing her damp flesh. Her breasts were pressed against him, soft, unbound. "I can't get enough of you, Jack." He pulled her toward the door.

"No." She drew back reluctantly, barely controlling her body's instincts. "I can't. I can't go sneaking around to 'do it' with you in corners."

He looked at her as if weighing her words, then opened the door and looked out. With a quick move he closed it again and turned the lock.

"A little high-handed, don't you think?" she said.

"Just talk?" he asked. His voice was deep and compelling, and she saw his arousal pressing against the fabric of his jeans, very much in evidence.

"Good." She dragged in a deep breath. "I need to ask you something."

He nodded once.

"What's been going on with you the last few days? Why have you been everywhere on the ranch but here? I . . . miss you." She looked away, embarrassed. "I know you have other responsibilities, but I know that you stopped handling the horses, that you're working the cattle, trading jobs with Ben just to stay away. It's me you've been avoiding, isn't it? Gray, you started this. Now what are you afraid of?"

She almost choked on the words, but she couldn't read the expression in his eyes. He just looked at her. Finally he made a whuffling sound that had to have been a laugh.

"Jack, I told you. When I'm around you, seeing you fifteen times a day . . . I want you all the time," he answered simply.

She turned red and an "Oh" slipped out.

"Seemed easier to be somewhere out of trouble." He touched her lips with a forefinger. "I ache for you."

Her eyes widened. She couldn't speak. He bent down and took her lips in a kiss that was unlike any she remembered. Her arms rose to clasp his big body, around his ribs to his strong back.

She murmured wordless, helpless sounds. "I thought . . ." she whispered. "I thought . . ." Tears crept from under her closed lids, and he hugged her hard, lifting her almost off the ground.

"Oh, babe," he groaned. His chest heaved, and he groaned again. For a long moment he simply held her tight.

"Come sleep with me," he murmured.

"No." A long sigh escaped her. "I can't. You know I can't."

"Why don't we tell them? Dammit." He straightened, pulling her with him. "Just get it out in the open and—"

"It's too soon," she said softly, but with conviction. "Besides, I thought you didn't want everyone on the place gossiping."

He scrubbed one hand roughly over his face. "Yeah, but that was before."

"Before what?"

"Before now," he said impatiently. Didn't she understand? he wondered. His feelings were as strong as they'd been at twenty-three. He wanted to share them with his family . . . with the world.

"So." He lifted her chin gently and tried to act like her answer didn't matter so very much. "How much time do you need?"

Her arms slipped around him and held him tight, her cheek to his warm shoulder. If she only made two major mistakes in her life, Jackie thought, that wasn't so terrible, was it? It was certainly more real joy than most people ever had.

But she was afraid that he would never really trust her, afraid that as soon as everyone knew about them, he would get bored and it would be over. Then there was that voice in the back of her head saying, "Take what you can get as long as you can get it."

"I don't know," she said, and she could feel his disappointment. But he rubbed her back in gentle resignation anyway.

It was the generosity of that melting gesture that finally pushed her to mumble, "The lock on that door any good?"

"What did you say, honey?"

She reached up on tiptoe and put her lips to his ear. "I said I want you inside me." Her tongue darted out to caress. "Right here, right now . . ."

He stared at her, her passion-dark eyes, her flushed cheeks, the pulse pounding at her throat. His mouth crushed hers in a hard, hungry seeking as his fingers tore at the belt of her robe. Grabbing one end in each hand, he dragged her back against him and ground his hips against her.

"Hurry," she whispered, pulling at his clothes.

He nipped at her breasts as he tore the robe off, then pulled her down to the soft rug. Her words had sent him crashing through any semblance of restraint.

"Oh, Lord . . ." he muttered. "I need you . . . can't . . . slow . . ." He groaned. "Can't . . ."

He threaded his fingers through the hair between her legs and down to her wet heat. His thumb circled and flicked in sweet friction as his mouth found her nipple. He drew deeply, and she cried out. His mouth moved to her other breast as he plunged a finger deep. In and out. Her hips moved with him, out of control.

"So hot for me, so wet," he said against her breast as her hips writhed and pushed against his hand.

"Come to me," she pleaded.

"Yes." With one deft twist, he turned her on her stomach and pressed his hard, burning arousal against the soft flesh of her bottom. His hands slid beneath her to her breasts as he rubbed his rigid length against her. Then he was kneading her buttocks, squeezing rhythmically. The heat from his hands warmed her, then singed her, as his thumbs made tiny circles and trailed down, slowly down.

"Please . . ." She squirmed against him, feeling every touch echo in the burning ache between her legs.

"Lift up."

As soon as she did, he was inside her, filling her with molten velvet, and she was shuddering with arousal, completely out of control. One of his hands pulled and teased a nipple while the other ran over her stomach possessively, over her abdomen, then lower, just above the soft triangle of hair, rotating against the rhythm he set.

Her fingers dug deep into the rug as she moaned and reached out blindly for something solid. Hands flailing, she found the legs of the daybed. She held on, trembling, as Gray plunged into her in fierce bursts, each thrust taking her higher than the last. "Don't . . . stop." Her head whipped back and forth.

"Hurry, Jack," he moaned, pushing as high into her womb as he could go. "You've got to—!"

Her neck arched back, but she couldn't get any closer, though the blazing, aching pleasure sparked with every plunge. Then Gray gave a low growl and grabbed one of her ankles shoving her leg forward and high against her hip. He changed his angle and thrust into her, and she screamed at the wild explosion of ecstasy.

He called her name as she closed around him, squeezing him tight in one volcanic convulsion after another.

"Tell me about the men who've been in your life since me," Gray asked her as he played with her fingers. They had been cuddled on the rug for a few minutes, silent, recovering.

She didn't answer.

"Jack?" He raised up on one elbow so that he could read her face. But there was nothing to see. Her expression was blank. "It's okay," he said. "I can handle it. I just want to know if they were good experiences or bad . . . what emotional baggage they left you with."

"No," she finally answered, carefully and precisely, as if she didn't lie naked in his arms. "I don't want to talk about that."

Ten

Merle and Dusty had finally gone to the lake, and Ben was in Dallas for a rodeo.

They were hardly gone four hours when Jackie found the flowers upstairs, next to her bedroom window. Wild flowers picked by his own hands. Much better than roses or orchids.

She ran down to the corral. He was there, walking Lucy for her. He looked at her and the blossoms she held.

He ran his hand exploringly over Lucy's wide stomach. The foal moved under his palm. "Shouldn't be much longer than a week or so now. Caro said the heartbeat's stronger."

"Oh, Junior." She sighed in relief and stroked the sleek coat herself. "This foal . . ." She pulled an oat stick from her pocket. "Daddy had some beautiful horses, but none of them had Lucy's bloodlines. Of course, it'll take a couple of years, and the Angus will have to support the ranch until we're ready, but I think we can make it."

"I've been waiting for you to tell me your plans." Gray's heart swelled as a wave of protectiveness overwhelmed him. She shouldn't have to struggle alone, ever again. "I want to be a part of them." He meant it as a commitment to partnership, the future.

Jackie, however, saw it as largesse, the promise of a loan, or the right word in the right ears.

She'd rather have flowers.

"Thank you for the flowers."

One eyebrow rose. "What flowers?"

"Oh. I thought . . ." She turned away, playing his game. "I'm looking for a cowboy who picks wild flowers."

"Um, well . . . I may know a fella like that."

"Yeah?" She started toward the barn, tugging Lucy after her.

"'Course, the information'll cost you."

She passed him with eyes downcast and boldly trailed one hand over his fly. "You don't say," she said, and left him there.

That night, they slept together in his wide bed. Just before dawn, Gray rolled over in his sleep and found her, like a present just waiting for him.

It was then Jackie discovered something she'd never realized. She had the ability to give, simply because Gray wanted what she gave. He responded so wholeheartedly to each brush of her fingers, each kiss warming his skin. That knowledge was as sharp and fine as any pleasure she'd ever known.

They finally slept again, spoon-curled, Gray breathing into Jackie's hair. She woke late, and panicked, then remembered the house was empty but for Gray.

Leaning back against his warmth, she saw that

he was still sleeping soundly. She smiled as she brushed her thumb over his soft lower lip.

His lips moved against her thumb, then captured it, drawing it in, sucking lightly. His eyes opened and blinked sleepily.

"You said it was because you were twenty-three," she whispered, and turned, pressing her belly against his hot arousal.

"I thought it was," he said around her thumb, and pushed back.

She laughed. He looked like a little boy. "That's not yours," she scolded, trying to draw her thumb back.

"Is now," he said, and kept nibbling.

She giggled in delight. "It's either that thumb or your breakfast." The fingers of her other hand raked the soft curling hair over his nipples.

He moved to settle himself on top of her, and gave a contented grunt. Still working his teeth tantalizingly on her skin, he mumbled, "I've got a craving for white silk."

The days passed honey slow, honey sweet. They had time now, time alone to share stories, secrets, to grow close. They watched TV and ate popcorn, necked on the couch, argued politics and favorite novels.

She smiled at the mess he made of his sock drawer, and he snickered at the way she couldn't just *sit* on the couch. She always had to have her shoes off and her feet tucked up under her. She gave him shoulder rubs, and he massaged her feet.

He liked to wake early, so he could catch her when she still had that soft, glazed look and her arms reached for him instinctively. He liked being able to get past her prickly defenses to the side of her she shared with no one else. They just didn't understand his woman.

He told her that he, too, had felt alone, as if people saw some parts of him, but were blind to others. Still, he thought himself an uncomplicated man, and Jackie couldn't disagree. He *liked* working horses, working cattle. He liked knowing that his physical labor affected his world. He found great satisfaction in it.

He and Jackie rode out to the site of Dusty's first rig with a picnic lunch, and tried to imagine what Dusty's life had been like then, with his dreams still so far away.

When Rand and Jenny invited Gray to dinner, he took Jackie. Jackie and Rand played audience as Gray and Jenny tried to outdo each other telling high school stories, neither of them the least embarrassed by things that would have made Jackie or Rand stomp from the room.

She had wondered, before that evening, if a Gray Burton, Jr. could ever really work with a Jackie Stone. That night, she watched Rand and Jenny together and thought of the ways their differences complemented each other. She decided those differences might be the very things that made them good together.

She studied Gray as they drove back to the ranch, thinking of his outside—the lanky good looks and strong arms and thick, muscular thighs, the beauty of his eyes and mouth; and his inside—the generosity of his nature, his kind ways and fairness of mind. The boy had become a man.

He caught her staring twice but didn't say anything. He just ground his teeth and pushed harder on the gas pedal. When they got home, he pulled her out of the truck and into his still-dark house. Without saying a word, he bent, lifted her over one shoulder, and took the stairs of his winding staircase two at a time while she laughed in delight.

Jackie shone with happiness, and Gray forgot to keep from staring at her when others were around. Pretty soon, the teasing at lunch grew from hints to cracks.

The boys had known something was going on for some time, and they appeared to be most fascinated with their power to make Gray blush. It happened with surprising regularity.

"No, no, no, sit *here*," they said, making sure he had the spot closest to the stove.

"Pass those taters down here, Billy. This boy's gonna need the energy."

"Brownies! Now who was it that's so crazy about brownies? Oh, yeah, these must be for you, boss. You don't mind if I take just one, do ya?"

Then there was the humming. Skinner and Bodean, older cowboys with grizzled cheeks and sweat-stained hats, had a conspiracy, humming country western love songs and snickering.

After that, Jackie pushed up her sleeves and took action on her own. She made her three-alarm chili at five bells and, with the first bites of dessert, she made laughing mention of the way cherry pie was said to disguise the taste of saltpeter.

It was a scene she would not soon forget, and it included the fastest, most polite exit from lunch she'd ever seen.

That evening Gray came into a kitchen filled

with the tantalizing aroma of rosemary, chicken, and roasting potatoes. He tossed his hat on a peg on the wooden rack. Without pausing, he grabbed her around the waist and whirled her in the air, laughing exultantly. Letting her slide down, he murmured, "Paddy's still scaring them with tales of vicious cooks he's known."

He carried her to a kitchen chair and set her down on his lap. Gathering the thick curling hair at her neck, he tugged until her lips were in line for his. "So, you've gotten into the habit of protecting me, huh?" His firm lips brushed hers, his breath caressed her. "I kind of like it." His teeth tugged at her full bottom lip. "I would have settled them down in my own way," he continued. She felt his taut belly move beneath her as he laughed. "But they were a sight to behold. I've never seen real fear on most of those faces . . ." He stopped laughing abruptly and kissed her witless.

Jackie had long since ceased to resist the man's slightest overture. She was a willing victim.

His hands slid up and down her arms as he studied her. She looked happy. "How come you look so pretty tonight?" he asked, nuzzling behind her ear. She wore a flower print apron over the pink sundress, and he could see that her legs were bare. He rested one hand on her knee. Soon restless fingers moved over the soft cotton, shaping flatness of bone, circling.

Gooseflesh rose at his touch, and she sighed.

"You look pretty too," she said. "Hungry?"

"Hmm." He made it an enthusiastic answer as his fingers slipped under the hem of her skirt to find the silky skin of her knee. His hand was hot against her cool flesh.

"It's good with us, isn't it?" she whispered wonderingly, her fingers pressed against his chest.

He pulled back and looked deep into her eyes. "Yes, it's good with us," he answered seriously. "Real good . . ." His voice trailed off as he bent to take her mouth.

Jackie watched his head angle down with anticipation. Her own lips softened and curved in a smile. But then she heard the squeak of the back door, and every muscle tensed.

Gray heard it too, and his arms tightened too late to hold her. He didn't care who it was. He and Jackie obviously weren't keeping any secrets anymore. He looked from where she had catapulted across the room and saw the last person he'd expected to see coming through that door.

It was Tom. Looking grim and purposeful and twenty pounds thinner, it was Tom come home.

Gray stood with a jerky motion so unlike him, Jackie thought he had tripped. Tom did nothing but stare at Gray for a long moment, then his gaze skimmed over to her. She blushed and smoothed her apron.

Tom was a couple of inches taller than Gray, six three or four, and a little broader across the shoulders. He was a Burton all right, and he might have been handsome, except for the fierceness of his expression.

"Gray," he finally said.

"Tom." Gray's voice sounded hoarse.

"I'm here to see Pop. I ran into Simon Burke in Florida. He told me Pop got gored."

"He's okay, now." Gray grasped the back of the chair and spoke slowly, each word sounded strangely weighted. "It was a long surgery, but he's recovering well. Getting restless, in fact. Merle took him up to the lake, but they should be back in a day or two. Ben's out of town too. He's bulldoggin' in Dallas." Gray looked over his shoulder at Jackie, wondering what to say next.

Tom's glance followed Gray's, and his expression softened. "Hi, Jackie. I didn't know you were here." He almost smiled. "How are you?"

"I'm fine, Tom. Glad you're back home." She smiled warmly.

He turned away like he would walk out. "Anyone livin' at—" He couldn't finish.

"I don't know how clean your house is," Gray said, "but it's waiting for you."

"Do you want some supper, Tom?" Jackie asked. "I've got a roast chicken."

"No," he answered harshly. "Thanks." He darted a look back over his shoulder. "I'll stay till Pop gets back. Then I'm gone."

Jackie sensed Gray's frustration, his urgency. She stepped forward and laid a hand on his arm before he could speak. Her other hand made a "wait" gesture.

Gray didn't want to, but he knew she was right. Now was not the moment for lengthy explanations. Tom was obviously having a hard enough time simply adjusting to being on the ranch.

Still, Gray couldn't just leave things as they were.

"We could use some help with the herd while you're here," he said, catching Tom just before he let go of the screen door.

"All right," Tom said without turning. Then he was gone, and the door banged shut.

Gray slept in her bed that night because she felt self-conscious about sleeping in his room with Tom on the ranch. He slept badly, tossing and turning, waking her a few times with urgent caresses.

She was glad he did. He was troubled, and she was happy to fill his mind and body with thoughts of her for diversion. Afterward, when they lay quietly, he spoke in a soft, liquid voice, rubbing her hair between his fingers.

"Tom knew everything when I was a kid. Pop would sic me on him, but he never complained, never got impatient. Taught me to ride, rope, to play ball. I never had a fight with him until you and I split. Then we never did anything else. He tried to talk to me about you—so many times. I wouldn't let him."

He was so quiet then, Jackie lifted her head from his shoulder to look at his face. His expression was strangely blank. He sniffed once and tightened his arm around her. "Screwed things up pretty good."

She cradled his face in her hand. Sitting back against the pillows, she tugged at him. "Come," she whispered.

With a simple sigh of relief, he came to her, resting his head upon her breast. Her hands feathered through his hair, over his temples. She kissed his forehead.

"Feels good," he murmured, cupping her breast with one hand. He raised his head just enough to kiss the soft flesh, then lay down again. "Sweet," he mumbled, and she held him, trying to swallow the lump in her throat as he fell asleep.

She stared through the dark and wondered what he'd say if he knew she might be pregnant.

Tom showed up for breakfast. He was polite to Jackie, but he hardly spoke to Gray. When they finished, they tromped out together, heading for the barn. Jackie walked to the screen door and pressed her fingertips lightly against it, watching them. The tension between them was evident in their stance, even at this distance.

Well, she thought resignedly, they'd have to work things out in their own way.

Just then Ben drove up in Gray's pickup. He skidded around the well and braked to a dusty stop. The next second he was out the door, running and yelling, "Bubba!"

Jackie laughed as Ben launched himself into his biggest brother's arms, wrapping arms and legs around Tom as if he weighted twenty pounds instead of a hundred and seventy, grabbing Tom's new-looking hat from his head and whooping like a banshee as he made circles in the air.

Jackie watched Gray as the other ranch hands came out to the yard in answer to the commotion. His face was devoid of expression, something she was beginning to associate with Tom's presence.

Tom dumped Ben on his feet and grabbed his hat back before he sent Ben's sailing. Paddy reached them first, greeting Tom warmly.

There was a strange absence of any more hollering and blackslapping as the boys collected in a circle, though Jackie knew well they were prone to big performances. In its place, hands were held out to be shaken, introductions made to those Tom didn't know.

Then Paddy asked Gray about assignments, a job that used to be Tom's, and everyone drifted back to work.

Lunch was pretty much as usual, except that no one knew where to sit, and no one told any jokes. No one looked at Gray or Tom, and everybody wanted out of there.

When Jackie went out to exercise Lucy later, she found Tom in the barn, currying one of the horses.

"'Lo." He gave a short nod.

"Hello," she said.

"Um, Jackie?" She looked up. "Can I ask you something?"

"Sure, Tom." Puzzled, she turned to face him.

"You been seein' Gray long?"

Blood rushed to her face, turning it fiery red, she was sure. Why she had to be born with skin that turned red as strawberries . . . She snatched at a breath as she looked back at Lucy. "Not . . . very long."

"You think you're gonna get married again?"

She whirled back, but before she could even open her mouth, he said, "Sorry. That was . . . I didn't mean . . . It's none of my business."

"What happened then was another lifetime ago, Tommy. Junior and I both made mistakes. I know I thought that things were either good or they weren't. I was too young to really know what a relationship meant. Phrases like 'work things out' and 'compromise' didn't even exist for me then."

Tom turned back to the horse he'd been tending, "I'm sorry about your dad. I liked Bill a lot."

Her eyes filled, and she blinked quickly. Gripping the wooden side of the stall, she said, "I'd stopped thinking about him. Like I just put it all on hold. I miss him."

"He left you a fine mare."

"Yes. You are, aren't you, girl?" She turned around and fed Lucy a carrot, then reached for the currycomb she'd taken from the tack room.

"I remember Bill talkin' about you taking over the place someday . . . about how much you loved horses, how good you were with them. He talked a lot about what you two could do together once you got the city out of your system."

"What?" She stood frozen. "What did you say?"

"Hey." He saw her face turn white, and walked over to her. "You all right?"

"I . . . What did you say?" She couldn't feel her legs.

"Come out of here." Tom took her elbow in a big, gentle hand and walked her to the tack room. He pushed her onto the bench there.

"I'm sorry," he said. "I didn't mean to upset you."

She still couldn't catch her breath. "You're saying my father wanted me to come home—to help him run the ranch?"

"Yeah." Tom looked puzzled. "He talked about how well you were doing in Houston, about how he was getting things in shape for you to come back home when you tired of the city."

"How can that . . . That can't be true." She looked down at the toes of her scuffed boots, embarrassed to have revealed the rift in her relationship with her father.

"Jackie, I didn't mean to bring up something that would throw you like this."

"I know, I know. Tell me again?" She looked up at him, tears spilling down her cheeks. "What did he say about me coming home?"

During dinner that night Jackie and Gray were both quiet. The tension between Gray and Tom lay like a boulder in the room.

Tom catalogued his past two years. He'd started a construction company in the boomtown of Orlando and done very well. Gray looked at Tom's face, at his stern expression, and wondered at the man he had become.

For once Jackie didn't sit for dinner. She couldn't have eaten anyway. She'd gotten a pregnancy test from the drugstore. Now it was definite.

As she started to clear their plates, Gray grasped her wrist. "Why don't you have somethin' to eat, Jack?"

"Not tonight." She couldn't even come up with a good lie. When she saw the concern in his eyes, though, she made the effort to smile. She felt his gaze on her back as she walked to the sink and knew her smile had fallen short.

She couldn't wait for dinner to be over to get away from the house. After she made coffee, she slipped through the living room and out the front door.

Eleven

Jackie raced down the now familiar trail through the long grass, up to the little hill in the meadow near the woods. At the crest of the hill she slipped to her knees, turned her face to the stars, and let the emotion sweep her. She felt the release of a strangling band of pressure she hadn't even known was there.

"Daddy," she whispered. "Oh, Daddy. What now?"

She sat down hard and curled over her knees. She couldn't tell Gray about the baby, not without hearing some words of love from him first. She didn't even know if he wanted children. Everything was so mixed up.

"Jack?" he said from behind her. He dropped beside her, wrapping his arms awkwardly around her. His voice seemed to come from some great distance. "Honey?"

He pulled her around to face him, and her heart beat against his as she wept with great, wrenching sobs.

"I miss my dad," she said. "I want him back!"

"It's okay." Gray rocked her, his own heart feeling torn. He knew she hadn't had a very good relationship with either of her parents. He thought of his own family and the warm acceptance from them he'd taken for granted growing up. He thought of the hurt look Jackie still got sometimes and held her tighter. "Cry it out, honey. Cry it out."

Gazing up at the stars, he held her until her sobs turned to great, halting sighs, then stopped altogether.

Jackie was too embarrassed to raise her head. Gray's chambray shirt was damp beneath her. Her tears had soaked it. Her face and lips felt swollen as she covered them with her hands and rubbed at the wetness. She didn't remember ever crying like that.

Weak. She'd acted weak and helpless and ridiculous. She hated that.

Gray felt her withdrawal as if she had moved many feet away. Shifting slightly, he pulled a white handkerchief from his pocket. Her hand shook a little as she reached for it, but he shifted again and tilted her face up to the moonlight. She closed her eyes tight, as if she could hide from him that way, and her fingers covered his as he dried her flushed cheeks. He let her take the handkerchief from him to blow her nose.

"I've drowned you." Her voice sounded husky as she swiped a shaky finger over the damp front of his shirt.

"Come on back to the house."

She looked down. "I'll be back later."

"You think I'm gonna leave you here, you're crazy."

She lay back in the prickly grass and found the Big Dipper. Eventually, she spoke into the quiet

night. "Tom told me my dad used to talk about—"
She swallowed, having trouble with the words.
"—about my coming home and running the ranch
with him."

Gray didn't say anything. He didn't know what
was wrong with that, until she went on.

"But Daddy never said anything like that to
me." It seemed the tears weren't dried, after all.
She felt them trace her temples into her hair. "I
wanted that from him, Junior. He's gone now, and
he never said it to me." She bit her lip and
stamped her fists hard into the earth. "Damn him!
He could tell Tom, but he couldn't tell me!"

He sat cross-legged beside her and knew he had
no words that could ease her pain. The only thing
he could do for her was to try to understand . . .
and be there.

Later, when they walked back, his arm came
around her shoulders. Hers anchored around his
waist two steps later.

When Ben appeared at lunch the next day, he
sported the shiny silver buckle he'd gotten for
roping. Everybody had heard the story of how he'd
won it except Jackie.

"I want to hear *every*thing," she told him.

Ben was so proud, he was even willing to run
the cowboy gauntlet for the sheer pleasure of
showing off. He had to know the treatment would
last for days, beginning with a round of teasing
comments and ending with terrible practical
jokes, all meant to keep the pigeon's head hat-
size. He obviously intended to enjoy the process.

So, he milked his story for all it was worth, then
sat back in his chair and waited for *the boys* to
have their do.

Tradition was important to a cowboy.

Jackie saw the first glimmer of brotherly camaraderie between Gray and Tom in the midst of that teasing. Almost without their volition, their eyes would meet across the table when Paddy hiked Ben's jeans higher and higher by that silver buckle for a *much* better look; or when iron-haired Rube asked Ben to tell again how he'd won it, listened, then asked questions as if he'd never heard the story in the first place. That was when Ben reached his limit, and despite their conflict, his two older brothers smiled at each other in wordless appreciation of the moment.

Gray and Tom rode together that afternoon. The pairing could have gone unnoticed, but it didn't.

The work was familiar. The air smelled like sun-warmed hide and weeds and dust. The heavens were brightest blue.

Gray waited for a couple of hours, until they were out there with their hands full, managing a small herd. The only words that had passed between them had been about their work. Gray looked at his brother riding his favorite horse, looking completely at home with his hat pulled low and his eyes squinting against the sun. Gray picked his moment and called across the wide backs of two irritated steers as they moved in a southerly direction.

"You gonna hit me if I tell you I know you never slept with Jack?"

Tom's head snapped up and he almost lost his seat when the bull calf wearing his rope gave a tug. He cursed and reeled the bawling animal in, leading the mother back to the herd. Looking up again, he saw Gray waiting for an answer.

"Why should you believe me now?" he yelled back.

"Why shouldn't I?" Gray bellowed, catching

sight of a straying calf. "Remember when Allie Johnson told everybody I got her pregnant? You believed me when I said I didn't. I thought you were the only one. And when Bumper told his daddy I was drivin' the night he wrecked the truck? You didn't have any trouble believing me then. Jack and I are working things out, Tom. We've talked a lot about those days." Finally he gave voice to the thought that had remained unspoken between them for years. "Before I saw Jack again, I needed somebody to blame. Maybe I made myself think the worst, because it was easier than thinking I'd made her so unhappy she would just leave. I'm sorry I didn't listen to you. I couldn't then."

"Jackie never wanted anyone or anything but you, Gray," Tom said quietly, looking at the horizon. "I was just someone she could talk to about the problems you two were having. She told me you were acting like her dad, hiding the bills, making all the decisions, leaving her out of things."

"I wanted to take care of her," Gray said, easily remembering those fierce feelings of protectiveness and possession. He still struggled with them.

"She told me something else once. She said she didn't need you to carry her through the mud." Tom looked at him. "She said she wanted to wade through it holdin' your hand." His gaze was serious. "I hope you let her do it this time, Gray. For both your sakes, I hope you're man enough."

Tom signaled his horse with his knees and hands to go after the calf, leaving Gray to think it over.

They didn't get home for another hour, but there were no more speeches. Side by side, they walked from the barn to the house. They washed up and came out of the bathroom together, then Gray opened the fridge and tossed Tom a beer without asking.

As they sat down to dinner, Ben told them how Rube and Paddy had kept on him all day. They started with peppermint oil on his saddle, then a girth so loose that when he tried to get back on Sadie, the whole saddle fell off, himself with it.

He laughed outright, telling how he couldn't throw a rope without the guys "pointin' and whoopin' and clappin' like they'd hit the mescal!"

Jackie was setting the rolls on the table when the doorbell rang. It was a telegram addressed to Gray.

"*Married in Mexico,*" he read. "*Happy as clams. I'm tan. Dusty's tanner. Must be recouped, won't leave me alone. It's just terrible. Home soon. Love—Merle & D.*"

"Hot damn!" Tom shouted as all three brothers grinned. "I bet it was her fishing that finally snared him." He caught his bottom lip in his teeth. "That woman." His delight was evident. "She probably made it a bet."

"Naw," Gray said. "She took a bottle of tequila!"

Ben was flat-faced serious, his voice slow and solemn. "You're talking about our mother."

They all hooted and guffawed and slapped one another's back.

"What d'you say after dinner," Tom suggested as he buttered a roll, "we all run down to McGinty's for a beer. We can celebrate, and I can see if this big talker's been practicin'."

"Great!" Ben was beaming. "Fresh meat!"

At Jackie's puzzled expression, Gray murmured, "Pool."

Tom reached over and ruffled Ben's hair so it stood straight up in back.

"You wish," he said, and turned to Jackie. "Okay with you, Jackie?"

"Sure," she answered. "It'll be good to get out for a little bit."

Gray didn't say anything. He was watching Tom, and the glint in his eye.

McGinty's had a sign out front that said NO OPEN TOED SHOES. NO MINORS. IF YOU GOT TO FIGHT—HIT 'EM OUTSIDE.

It was a pretty lively bar, even on a Thursday night, with a four-piece country band and a dance floor on one side, pool tables on the other, and tables and chairs everywhere else. The waitresses wore jeans and boots, with T-shirts that said McGinty's Armadillo Beer. Sawdust and peanut shells littered the floor.

Ben put down a row of quarters to reserve a table, and they found bar stools nearby. Tom ordered four beers, but Jackie touched his arm and corrected him.

"Seven-up, please, Tommy."

He gave her an interested glance and got their drinks.

They toasted to Merle and Dusty's happiness, then Tom asked Jackie how she had liked living in Houston and the U of H.

Ben and Gray started a pool game while Tom and Jackie traded college horror stories. It was the first time Gray had heard Tom laugh aloud in a long time. He stopped midshot just to watch.

They were sitting with their backs to the bar, and Tom had spread his arms out along the smooth wood on either side of him. One arm was behind Jackie, the other held a longneck. Jackie's face was flushed with pleasure as she laughed at one of Tom's stories.

Gray looked at Jackie's yellow T-shirt and jeans,

at the way she pushed her hair back over her shoulder, the way she held her glass. He looked at Tom's head tilted in her direction. His brother was sending him a message . . . a test.

He lost the game and returned to the bar. Dropping the base of his cue on the floor, he leaned the tip Tom's way. When Tom took it, Gray pulled Jackie's glass from her hand, placed it carefully upon the bar, and tugged her off the stool.

"Dance with me," he said in a tone she'd never heard him use before.

It wasn't a request, but it wasn't an order.

He pulled her close in time for a fast two-step, his eyes never leaving hers. Then from nowhere, Tom cut in.

"Brother." He nodded to Gray and swept her away.

He was a big man, with wide shoulders. He was the first Burton she'd seen who didn't eat for three, but he still probably had twenty pounds on Gray.

He was a good dancer, but his touch at her back felt unfamiliar. The hand holding hers was warm and purposeful. Too purposeful.

"Do you mind your dad marrying the cook?" she asked tentatively.

"Merlie?" He looked surprised. "I've been waiting for it. We all have."

Jackie looked over at the bar and saw Gray leaning there, legs crossed negligently at the ankle, his hat tipped back, watching them. She saw him turn and order another beer. Looking back at Tom, she saw a twinkle in his eye, as if he'd been waiting for a reaction.

She pursed her lips. "Don't you think you two are a little old for this game?"

"Naw." Tom grinned. He was obviously enjoying himself.

"Well I am." She stomped on his foot, hard, and she did it on purpose. They both stumbled, and Jackie pushed back. "I don't think I want to play the bone between two howlin' dogs." She spun away to find Gray standing behind her, looking like a bashful John Wayne.

"Want to take a walk?" he asked.

"*That* depends on your attitude, Junior." She gave him a feisty stare. "You can act like a ten-year-old gunfighter, or you can show me the stars."

He ducked his head down, trying to hide how she pleased him. Taking off his hat, he kept staring at the toes of his boots. "I'd like to show you the stars, ma'am."

"Fine." She marched to the front door, still refusing to be charmed.

Gray didn't even waste a look on Tom.

"You could slow down, you know," he said as he followed her outside. "You'll never see a falling star while you're goin' fifty miles an hour."

At his words she did slow down. They were walking across grass by that time, and she came to a stop with her head bent down. He reached out to stroke the soft hair gleaming sliver in the moonlight. With the second stroke, his hand settled around the nape of her neck.

"I thought for a minute you two were going to get in a fight back there," she said as she turned to him.

He tugged her to his chest. "Naw. Tommy was just trying to prove a point."

"What do you mean?" Her voice was muffled against him. She moved her head to draw his scent deep inside her. He smelled so good.

"Oh, I don't know. Maybe that I'd never had any reason to be jealous . . . and what an ass I'd been. Something like that."

"You made the right choice, coming outside with me," she teased him, kissing the vee of hair-covered chest that showed above the first button of his shirt.

He glanced down, and his arms tightened. She lifted her head, and his mouth found hers in a kiss that was deep and possessive and reassuring.

His hand cupped her breast as if he held her heart, and hers found his jaw. When the kiss ended, he looked into her eyes and smiled.

"Want to go back inside and dance with me?" he asked.

She nodded, and their hands swung back and forth between them with each step. "Are you happy about Merle and Dusty?"

"Long overdue."

He brushed his thumb against her palm and pushed in the door with his free hand. The band was playing a ballad, and she clasped her arms around his neck as his hands rested on her hips. He pulled her closer until he could feel her body curving pliantly against him. He pressed a kiss behind her ear and whispered, "Babe."

Heat soaked through her, and her fingers tangled in his soft hair. How she loved this man and his warm, winning ways.

Rough cheek pressed to smooth temple, they slow danced, and Jackie felt things she could not name—joy and a strange assurance that someone cared for *her*. A look of understanding passed between them as the music stopped. They crossed the room to the pool table, where they found Tom cleaning up, while Ben grinned and shook his head.

"The construction story's a scam," Ben said. "I know Tom's been hustlin' pool halls in Florida all this time."

Tom looked up long enough to shoot an amused glance at his youngest brother, then he plugged the lonely eight ball and straightened in satisfaction. He looked at Gray and Jackie, smiling at the way they were together.

"So when you two gettin' married?"

Gray was going to make some light comment about doing his own asking in his own time, until he looked at Jackie and saw her face.

"Time to go, isn't it?" she said, looking down at her watch. "I really need to get back to check on Lucy." Paddy had told her the previous evening that Lucy was waxing. She'd be in labor in less than two days—and a week early.

Tom and Ben both looked at Gray, who gave away nothing.

Back at the ranch, Jackie went right to the barn. Paddy was in the birthing stall with Lucy.

"Here ye are," he said. "Her water broke and her milk's come in." He spoke mater-of-factly as he bent before Lucy's swollen side.

Fear and excitement churned through Jackie as she looked over her shoulder, hoping that Gray would be there. He was, on the other side of the wooden partition, his forearms resting casually on the edge, chin supported on fists.

"You can call Caro from the tack room," he said, "but you're probably going to want to freeze that milk for the foal before too much goes wasting."

Jackie was suddenly so nervous, she felt like she was thinking through a fog. She crouched to stroke Lucy's nose and spoke over her shoulder to Gray. "You know what to do?"

"Come on, I'll show you." He opened the stall for her.

She turned to Paddy. "You'll stay with her?"

Paddy nodded and murmured soothingly to Lucy. He glanced at Gray. "Y'can bring the kit back with you."

In the tack room Gray handed her the telephone receiver, then dialed when he saw how her hands shook. He watched her face as she spoke to the vet's service.

"Do you know what kind of case she's on? What about her partner? Oh . . . all right. Thank you." Her face was white as she gave the phone back to Gray. "Caro's out on call in Carson. Her partner's on vacation."

He replaced the receiver and pulled her into his arms. She was stiff. "Paddy and I have pulled more foals and calves than either of us can even remember." Her chin curled over his shoulder.

"I have a bad feeling, Junior," she whispered. "A scary feeling." Her voice choked. "I haven't had a lot of luck with babies."

Pain shot through his chest, and his arms tightened convulsively. He closed his eyes and willed her some of his strength. "It'll be all right. We'll make it be."

When she settled down beside the mare, he brought blankets and pillows from the tack room closet. She grinned, her nerves showing through.

"Thanks."

He grinned back and hooked his arm around her neck to steal a kiss. "Welcome."

The powerful contractions started a half hour later—at the same time that Ben tumbled into the barn and yelled for Gray.

"Hush now, lad." Paddy met him in the aisle. "Yer brother has his hands full at the moment."

Ben looked into the stall and saw Lucy down.

Jackie was holding her head, and Gray was swabbing her with antiseptic. Without turning, Gray demanded, "What is it, Ben?"

Ben lowered his voice. "Max crashed his fence."

"What!" That was Paddy, mad as a stung bee. "That black behemoth has done it again?" He threw his cap to the ground and stamped in place like Max himself. "If that bloody Angus is terrorizin' the stock again, we'll be eatin' steak by breakfast!"

Gray laughed. "Remember to save Pop the biggest slice, Paddy."

"Och, the devil. Well, one of us had best be there to help the boy, and it doesn't look as though ye need me here atall."

"The boy?" Ben was indignant.

"Where's Tom?" Gray recapped the antiseptic.

"I couldn't find him," Ben answered.

"Go on, then." Gray was busy feeling the contraction occurring under his hand.

Jackie was finally calming. Gray was the kind of man who inspired confidence. She watched him work and stroked Lucy's fine neck, talking softly to her.

"She's beginning to present," Gray said, watching carefully. "There you go, girl." In a matter of seconds, though, Jackie saw his face change.

Trying to sound calm so her voice wouldn't upset Lucy, she spoke his name.

"She's presenting her nose and right foot," he answered. "No left. If the foal comes on the next contraction, she'll be torn and the foal may be damaged." Jackie's heart slammed against her ribs. Gray looked up at her, and she read his own anxiety. "I need to go in."

"Why don't you let Jackie do it?" Tom asked from outside the stalls.

Gray looked up at Tom, then back at Jackie. He nodded. "If she wants." He kept his gaze on her, his eyes steady and confident. "Lubricant is in the kit. Tom will hold her head, and I'll help you here. We need to hurry. If a contraction hits while you're in there, you might do more damage than good."

Time seemed to slow after that. Jackie touched the velvet nose once more and moved to the kit. In a blur of motion, Tom poured antiseptic over her hands and put a "sleeve" on her that came up over her elbow. Once in place, the glove was coated with a clear jelly. Then she was on her knees beside Gray.

"Here y'go." Gray took a breath. "You'll feel for the hoof. There may be resistance, but you've got to straighten it. Understand?" She nodded. "Go on and hurry. That's it, past the right hoof."

Her hand was squeezed so tight, she doubted she would get in far enough. But then she felt it. Small, rounded, and oval. Grasping the hoof, she tugged, but it wouldn't move.

"I can't budge it," she gasped.

"Pull harder! Come on, Jack, or she'll be torn. Keep working it."

She was sure it wouldn't go, and then, she could have sworn the foal helped. The hoof moved. As soon as the leg was straight, she pulled out and the next contraction began. This time Jackie could see that the foal presented itself properly, feet and nose. Only a moment later, the foal was delivered. Struggling to his feet, he wobbled to his mother.

Miraculous, Jackie thought as she stared.

"A colt." Gray grinned at Tom. "Out of Doc Bar!"

"We did it!" Jackie felt the dampness on her cheeks, but her smile was stunning as she pulled both brothers to her in a fierce, dancing hug. They rocked together, laughing for a long time.

She named him Bar None and spent hours just staring at him that first week. As she watched, she would unconsciously rub her palm over her stomach, thinking about the beauty of her own child growing within her. She prayed that nothing would go wrong this time.

Dusty and Merle finally arrived home, honking madly as they rounded the drive, tires spitting gravel and dust into the usual cloud behind them. Before either of them was able to open a door, they were surrounded by a whistling, yahooing mob. The bride and groom looked tanned and fit and indecently happy as they waded through to each other's side.

Somebody yelled something about "Hurricane Merle," and Dusty laughed and pulled her close for a Rhett Butler-bend-her-over kiss. Just before their lips met, he looked up and said, "Six months of bein' manly and playin' hard to get got me nowhere, fellas! If I'd known all I had to do was show her my secret fishin' spot, Max and I wouldn't have gone to such desperate measures to get her attention." Then he wowed Merle and everybody else with a kiss of epic proportions. "But she's still worth her weight in catfi—" He broke off when he saw his two oldest sons riding toward him. The mob parted to make a path, and he released Merle before he strode toward them, a fierce light in his eye.

They were on the ground when he reached them.

"Pop." Tom smiled in warm welcome, the shadows in his face softened.

"Boy." He nodded to Tom, then looked at Gray, studying. He nodded again, somehow satisfied.

"Good you're home," he said, turning back to Tom, "Made it just in time to kiss your wicked stepmother."

"My prince." Merle rolled her eyes behind him as Tom and Dusty backslapped each other.

Their champagne was beer, and all through dinner Merle kept cracking dirty jokes at Dusty's expense, while he looked on, wise and enigmatic. There was something damn sexy about that look, Jackie thought, and wondered if she'd see Gray wear it in thirty years or so.

When dinner was done, Merle stood to help Jackie clear the dishes. As she bent over for Dusty's plate, he snagged her around the waist.

"Boys," he said, "You're gonna have to go a far piece to find you a girl with sass like this."

"Oh, I don't know," Gray said as he pulled Jackie, her arms full of rattling plates, down onto his lap. "Not so far . . ."

"Junior!" Jackie protested, red-faced and indignant.

"Maybe I already got her," he went on as he rocked her, plates and all.

Jackie looked around wildly. The walls were closing in as Tom laughed and said, "So, when *is* the wedding?"

She heard the plates crash before she felt them slip from her hands. She was dizzy, but that didn't stop her from shooting off Gray's lap and out of that room.

Gray searched the house, but there was no sign of Jackie. From her bedroom window, he finally saw her. She was doing laps in the pool.

Circling around, he waited for her in the pool house. He tried to gather his thoughts, letting his emotions settle as he wondered at the best approach.

He turned off one of the lamps and pushed aside the curtain at the window to watch her. She swam with speed and economy of motion. But then she stopped midlength and put her hands over her face. He hesitated, then started out after her, throwing open the door. She was already out of the pool. She marched straight to the pool house, sweeping right by him and into the bathroom.

"Jack?" He splayed one hand against the door closed against him. "Honey?"

No answer.

"Come on, honey. Open the door. We need to talk." Seconds passed. At last the door opened wide and she stood before him in her white terry robe, her golden eyes liquid with tears, her expression controlled. The look she wore was the same one he'd seen the day her car crashed into the well. He thought of it as her "I can take it—I can take anything" look.

He hated it.

"What's up, Jack?"

"Nothing," she said in a voice like dull metal. "It's about time for me to go home, that's all."

Something slammed his gut. He couldn't think, couldn't move. "What?" The word slipped from him.

"I have to in a few weeks anyway."

"Make me understand, Jack."

"How could you possibly understand, Junior? You belong. No one tells you you're not good enough. You've proven yourself. I haven't *done* things—haven't been allowed to—not what I want. Someone's always told me what I can and can't do, or the money's not there. Well this is my chance, to prove to myself and the world that I can be what I want and be a success. I've got Lucy and the foal. Bandolino can be a big prizewinner, I know it. I'm going to turn my ranch around. I have to do it. I've dreamed about it too long. And I'm damned if I'll have people saying I slept with you to get it!"

"Fine, then. But let me help. Let's do it together."

"No! You don't get it. *I* have to do it, *I* have to make it work."

"Why?" He was angry, so angry he felt his vision cloud. "Because you want to prove yourself to a dead man? That's stupid, Jackie! What about me, what about this baby?"

Jackie was frozen, and she would stay frozen for all time, she was certain. Then, after a few moments, she began to breathe again.

"How . . . when did you know?" She couldn't help the tremor in her voice.

"Do you think I don't know you?" he answered quietly. "I've spent a thousand nights since you left me wondering why I didn't know then. Did you think I wouldn't see the changes now?" He went on, stalking her. "Your nipples are darker, and they're a little bigger. Your breasts feel full of life and," he whispered, "very, very sensitive." He sighed at the discomfort he was causing himself and went on. "Your soft, sweet little belly has hardened, and my lips know the difference."

"No," she said, a last denial at all the things she could not control.

"We're together every night, Jack," he said finally. "I count the days just like you."

At that, she buried her face in her hands. *Of course he had known. Of course.*

"I'm not ready for this," she said.

"Did you think I was just going to wait until you felt like you were ready? Love doesn't work that way. I don't work that way. I wasn't ready to feel all this again, either, Jack. But I'm not a man who can be turned on and off like a switch."

Gray heard the echo of his own words, and panic settled in his chest. Things were getting out of hand. He wouldn't let her do this to them. It was too important.

"Let's be realistic, Graham."

She'd called him "Graham," a voice inside his head shouted. She went on, sounding like someone else.

"How long could it have lasted? I'm not really up to your speed, and we both know it. But you'll be able to see the baby whenever you want, and you won't be tied down—"

"So this is about your damned insecurity?" he interrupted in a roar. "You think you're not important to me? That what we have will just slip away? You think I don't want my own child?"

"I think that's what you want most," she whispered, tears spilling from her eyes. "And I can't stand to have to wonder the rest of my life if you would have wanted just me."

Gray's eyes turned dark and dangerous. One hand grasped her waist, dragging her closer, while the other slid inside her robe and cupped her breast possessively. Just that touch created a familiar ache low in her belly, and her hips arched, searching for his. His thumb circled lightly over her nipple, and he felt the thudding of her heart.

"You love me. I know you do." His voice was low and grating. "I want to hear you say it to me. Say it."

"Yes."

"Say it!"

"I love y—" but the words were cut off by his fierce kiss.

Her hands pressed against his chest, and he tightened his grip on her waist, groaning into her mouth. She could feel him trembling as he pulled away.

"Then let me in," he said. "All the time you've been back, you've held me away from you—away form the most important parts of you. *Trust* me in your life, Jack. Trust me to be your partner. To hell with who says what. We know what the truth is. I love you. I've never said that to another woman. I love *you*. Marry me." His gaze locked with hers. "Don't you feel the rightness of this?" And his mouth branded her as his words echoed through her.

She pulled away at last. "Junior, do you know what you're doing?" Her hands cupped his face. Could he mean it? She shook her head. "No, we don't have to do that."

"Chance it." His voice was flat and without humor. He sealed his intent with another kiss, this one gentle, coaxing, and deeply erotic.

"We're good together, remember?" he whispered against her lips. He looked reckless and angry. He looked beautiful.

She dizzied once more, raising her arms around his neck. He reached down, slipped through the overlapping material of her robe, and touched the soft curls between her legs. She murmured in confusion.

Dropping to his knees before her, Gray tugged at her sash. "Tell me you don't remember what you feel when I'm inside you. Tell me you don't remember this." He kissed her silky belly again and again, his hands at her slender hips, his voice full of need, full of passion. "You belong with me. We belong together."

Before she could take another shallow breath, he had slipped his hands between her legs to grab her bottom. His hot mouth found her, and she flinched again at the intensity.

"Junior." Her whisper drifted down to him. She felt her body quake, and her head fell back in abandon. She knew he was using unfair advantage to make his point, and still, she couldn't make herself stop him.

Her hands pressed into the cool wall behind her, and her breathing was labored. Her knees wouldn't have held her without his support and, within moments, she was pushed right to the edge.

Lord, Gray thought, he loved that he could make her crazy. He nuzzled the blond curls and made a noise that vibrated against her. Whimpering his name, Jackie lost all sense of place and time. Her fingers shook as they found his hair. They threaded through it until she felt the scrape of his teeth on her most sensitive flesh, and she convulsed against him, gasping, every nerve exploding into streaming, golden pleasure.

There was no time to recover, no time to think before his fingers slid deep into her swollen heat and his mouth found her again.

"Please, no . . . Junior . . . " *Revenge,* she thought.

"Yes, feel it. Feel my mouth," he whispered tantalizingly. "You're so soft, taste like honey." His fingers started a driving rhythm that drew a low sound from her throat. "That's right, moan for me, baby . . . So hot."

His words aroused her as much as his burning

touch, and her fists clenched helplessly. Then her fingers spread through his hair and caressed the straining cords of his neck.

Her hips twisted and pushed as she surrendered to him. Her shaking hands stroked silky skin and hard muscle. She couldn't fight anymore.

He began to draw upon her in a scalding suction, two fingers still buried deep inside her, and she was thrown into a wild explosion that electrified every nerve and left her sobbing in pleasure. He waited only a moment before his hand cupped her.

His mouth went to a hard nipple, scraping lightly as the heel of his hand pressed and rotated. "Junior," she pleaded, but he only moved to her other breast, trailing wet kisses around and around, then finally closing over the pebbled bud.

Just satisfied, she burned.

He stood and kissed her mouth with a dark, soul-reaching kiss that had her running her hands over him in reckless longing.

He steadied her against the wall and, in one swift motion, pushed his jeans and briefs away. His eyes darkened and grew slumberous as he studied her. He smoothed her hair from her face and then brushed the tears from her cheeks.

"You drive me out of my mind," he said hoarsely. "But you belong to me, and I belong to you. Say it!" He bent, grasping her thighs.

"Yes!" she answered.

He lifted her and filled her with brilliant heat. Her legs wrapped around him and locked behind as she tightened her grip on his neck. He pressed her hard and rhythmically into the wall, his hands controlling her with a strength that awed her, pushing her up in fast, desperate motions, then retreating, letting her slide back.

Turning toward the small daybed, he walked in slow motion, savoring each shift of position and the sounds she made, until he lowered her in painstaking inches to the mattress.

"Feel me inside you," he whispered, drawing back and out, until she whimpered. " . . . Yes."

Murmuring her name, he pushed again into her swollen heat and began a slow, driving rhythm that had her crying out. Her breasts moved with every thrust, and he brushed her nipples, heightening the ache. Then he squeezed her bottom, pressing moist, openmouthed kisses wherever he could.

Reaching down, his hand found her and slid over her, then rolled the tender flesh between his fingers. She was on fire. She shook her head wildly before she crashed through wave after wave of devastating pleasure.

Gray's throat worked as he struggled for control. Finally, he released a long breath and thrust deeply, over and over, muscles quivering. Suddenly, he stilled above her.

Her eyes opened in alarm. She looked up at his twisted features and asked quickly between gasps, "What . . . Is it . . . your knee?"

"Don't move," he groaned. "Oh, sweet heaven, don't move."

She froze, searching his face, hoping to find some clue to his pain. He gave a deep breath and withdrew almost completely, his expression agonized. Without conscious thought, her inner muscles clenched, trying to hold him. He made a noise that was part groan, part laugh, and grasped her even more tightly.

When he couldn't hold back his own release a moment longer, he lunged once, twice, and exploded with a ragged cry.

Afterward, lying in the warmth of Gray's arms, she turned to nuzzle his shoulder. "I love the way you touch me. No, it's not enough to say I love it." She pushed closer to him. "The way you look when you touch me, the way you make me feel. I want to tell you how it makes me different." She glanced down, and was disconcerted by the picture she made sprawled out on the daybed. She sat up in a rush.

He scowled up at her. "Don't tell me you're sorry."

"Oh, Junior." She turned back to him. Combing back the damp hair from his forehead, she smiled. "How could I be? I love you so much."

His eyes closed in pleasure at her words. He'd been afraid he had lost her again.

"I can't believe this is me," she went on. "I mean, I don't act like this—at least I haven't acted like this since I was eighteen—and I'd be horrified if anyone knocked on that door." She curled back into his arms. "But I can't say I'm sorry. You're wonderful, and you make me feel . . . wonderful."

After a moment, she pulled herself back out of his arms. She stood and took her time straightening her robe, getting the sash exactly right. When she turned to him again, he was standing, hands on his hips, still beautifully naked. She knew he had made love to her because it was the way he best communicated his love. She might have liked it if he had played the poet. But her man would ever be a man of action. He had given her his poem, and it had been splendid.

"Remember that then," he said. "Remember how I make you feel." His eyes darkened. "And remember this. I've only been truly happy when you're in my life. I need you there, Jack, to have you in my bed at night. I can't sleep without you.

I need the smell of you in my head, the sight of your sweet smile, your yellow hair. I won't let you run away from me again. We're a family. You and me and our baby. I'll make you happy, too, Jack, whatever it takes."

So, she thought, overwhelmed. He'd given her the words, after all.

She had to warn him, but she didn't have to look at him while she did it. "I might not be able to carry this baby to term, Junior. Have you thought about that?"

His hand was warm upon her shoulder as he turned her to him. The look in his eyes gladdened her soul. "Whatever happens, Jack, we're in this together."

Her heart bounced happily, but she wasn't finished.

"I'd still want to live at my ranch, and I can't promise not to be a little territorial. That won't change overnight." Blood rushed to his cheeks, and his blue eyes glowed. She tried to think of the other things he'd hate. "I wouldn't take any of your money either." He stepped forward, stalking her. She held up a hand to ward him off. "And if I ever caught you with another woman, I'd never, ever forgive you."

He hauled her into his arms and sighed deeply, happily. "You, my girl, will have to learn to share— Oh, not me." He held up a hand in defense and laughed. "But other things. The baby, my money, your ranch. Partners, remember? We'll live there, and I'll put up with you if you put up with me. And I'll love you, Jack. I'll make sure you know you're loved. I'll make you cry with pleasure and glow with pride at what we've done together." He kissed her hard, then soft. Pulling back, he looked down at her and asked, "Deal?"

Staring at him, Jackie couldn't believe what she held in her arms. He was right when he'd said he'd never lied to her. She knew the value of his word. She gave him a hard kiss, then a soft one, and took her life in her own two hands.

Epilogue

"Don't push, Jack, wait . . . just a bit longer, it's almost over." Gray dabbed at her forehead with a cool washcloth and let her crush his other hand.

"I have to *push*!" Her face contorted, and his heart with it.

Gray looked at the doctor, hoping, waiting. She shook her head. "Not yet, Jackie, but very soon. Hold on, you're doing fine, just fine."

But while the doctor was occupied, Jackie was working up a rage at Gray.

"I want to push, you cretin," she shouted at him. "Haven't women been doing this for five billion years! While men sit around saying 'Don't push!'"

Gray opened his mouth, but had no answer. At least she was still crushing his hand, he thought, instead of pushing. Finally the doctor said, "All right, here we go, Jackie. Now, with the next contraction you can push."

But Jackie couldn't hear her. Gray was her only link to life and earth. He realized it in a single startling flash and grinned.

"Okay, my honey girl, it's our time. When you feel it, push. Push like crazy! Our baby's comin', and I want to catch him. Can you let me go long enough to do that, or do you want me here?"

Her face looked terrible in pain, and beautiful. He saw her struggle to understand his words, a sight he would never forget as she said, "Be there . . ."

Moments later, their son was born, and Gray's were the first arms to hold him. At the doctor's direction, he placed him upon his mother's stomach. Then he wept like a babe, Jackie's hand in his hair.

Watching his wife nurse their child, Gray felt a deep satisfaction with the world and life in general. There was just one little thing he wanted to clear up.

"Jack?" he began softly.

She smiled at him, her happiness glowing in her eyes.

"Will you tell me something?"

"Anything," she said, distracted by the baby.

"Who hit you that night at the Lone Star?"

Jackie swallowed hard. Then, knowing her love, knowing how he valued the truth, knowing how he could bleed, she did the only thing she could.

"Are you sure you really want to know?" she asked seriously.

"Yes, dammit! I really want to know."

"All right." She drew it out for two beats. "I slipped and hit the back of a chair when we were running from Hank that night."

"You . . ." He blinked. "And all this time you let me wonder if . . ."

"You always have been too cocky, cowboy." She

gave him a sly glance, filled with laughter and other warm things.

His indignation turned to a grin. "Yeah." He nuzzled her cheek in a sweet caress. "And ain't you a lucky girl."

THE EDITOR'S CORNER

There's a lot to look forward to from LOVESWEPT in October—five fabulous stories from your favorites, and a delightful novel from an exciting new author. You know you can always rely on LOVESWEPT to provide six top-notch—and thrilling—romances each and every month.

Leading the lineup is Marcia Evanick, with **SWEET TEMPTATION,** LOVESWEPT #570. And sweet temptation is just what Augusta Bodine is, as Garrison Fisher soon finds out. Paleontologist Garrison thinks the Georgia peach can't survive roughing it in his dusty dinosaur-fossil dig—but she meets his skepticism with bewitching stubbornness and a wildfire taste for adventure that he quickly longs to explore . . . and satisfy. Marcia is at her best with this heartwarming and funny romance.

Strange occurrences and the magic of love are waiting for you on board the **SCARLET BUTTERFLY,** LOVESWEPT #571, by Sandra Chastain. Ever since Sean Rogan restored the ancient—and possibly haunted—ship, he'd been prepared for anything, except the woman he finds sleeping in his bunk! The rogue sea captain warns Carolina Evans that he's no safe haven in a storm, but she's intent on fulfilling a promise made long ago, a promise of love. Boldly imaginative, richly emotional, **SCARLET BUTTERFLY** is a winner from Sandra.

Please give a big welcome to new author Leanne Banks and her very first LOVESWEPT, **GUARDIAN ANGEL,** #572. In this enchanting romance Talia McKenzie is caught in the impossible situation of working very closely with Trace Barringer on a charity drive. He'd starred in her teenage daydreams, but now there's bad blood between their families. What is she to do, especially when Trace wants nothing less from her than her love? The answer makes for one surefire treat. Enjoy one of our New Faces of 1992!

Ever-popular Fayrene Preston creates a blazing inferno of desire in **IN THE HEAT OF THE NIGHT,** LOVESWEPT #573. Philip Killane expects trouble when Jacey finally comes home after so many years, for he's never forgotten the night she'd branded him with her fire, the night that had nearly ruined their lives. But he isn't prepared for the fact that his stepsister is more gorgeous than ever . . . or that he wants a second chance. An utterly sensational romance, with passion at its most potent—only from Fayrene!

In Gail Douglas's new LOVESWEPT, **THE LADY IS A SCAMP,** #574, the lady in the title is event planner Victoria Chase. She's usually poised and elegant, but businessman Dan Stewart upsets her equilibrium. Maybe it's his handshake that sets her on fire, or the intense blue eyes that see right inside her soul. She should be running to the hills instead of straight into his arms. This story showcases the winning charm of Gail's writing—plus a puppet and a clown who show our hero and heroine the path to love.

We end the month with **FORBIDDEN DREAMS** by Judy Gill, LOVESWEPT #575. When Jason O'Keefe blows back into Shell Landry's life with all the force of the winter storm howling outside her isolated cabin, they become trapped together in a cocoon of pleasure. Jason needs her to expose a con artist, and he also needs her kisses. Shell wants to trust him, but so much is at stake, including the secret that had finally brought her peace. Judy will leave you breathless with the elemental force raging between these two people.

On sale this month from FANFARE are three exciting novels. In **DAWN ON A JADE SEA** Jessica Bryan, the award-winning author of **ACROSS A WINE-DARK SEA,** once more intertwines romance, fantasy, and ancient history to create an utterly spellbinding story. Set against the stunning pageantry of ancient China, **DAWN ON A JADE SEA** brings together Rhea, a merperson from an undersea world, and Red Tiger, a son of merchants who has vowed revenge against the powerful nobleman who destroyed his family.

Now's your chance to grab a copy of **BLAZE,** by bestselling author Susan Johnson, and read the novel that won the *Romantic Times* award for Best Sensual Historical Romance and a Golden Certificate from *Affaire de Coeur* "for the quality, excellence of writing, entertainment and enjoyment it gave the readers." In this sizzling novel a Boston heiress is swept into a storm of passion she's never imagined, held spellbound by an Absarokee Indian who knows every woman's desires. . . .

Anytime we publish a book by Iris Johansen, it's an event—and **LAST BRIDGE HOME** shows why. Original, emotional, and sensual, it's romantic suspense at its most compelling. It begins with Jon Sandell, a man with many secrets and one remarkable power, appearing at Elizabeth Ramsey's cottage. When he reveals that he's there to protect her from danger, Elizabeth doesn't know whether this mesmerizing stranger is friend or foe. . . .

Also on sale this month in the Doubleday hardcover edition is **LADY DEFIANT** by Suzanne Robinson, a thrilling historical romance that brings back Blade, who was introduced in **LADY GALLANT.** Now Blade is one of Queen Elizabeth's most dangerous spies, and he must romance a beauty named Oriel who holds a clue that could alter the course of history.

Happy reading!

With warmest wishes,

Nita Taublib
Associate Publisher
LOVESWEPT and FANFARE

OFFICIAL RULES TO WINNERS CLASSIC SWEEPSTAKES

No Purchase necessary. To enter the sweepstakes follow instructions found elsewhere in this offer. You can also enter the sweepstakes by hand printing your name, address, city, state and zip code on a 3" x 5" piece of paper and mailing it to: Winners Classic Sweepstakes, P.O. Box 785, Gibbstown, NJ 08027. Mail each entry separately. Sweepstakes begins 12/1/91. Entries must be received by 6/1/93. Some presentations of this sweepstakes may feature a deadline for the Early Bird prize. If the offer you receive does, then to be eligible for the Early Bird prize your entry must be received according to the Early Bird date specified. Not responsible for lost, late, damaged, misdirected, illegible or postage due mail. Mechanically reproduced entries are not eligible. All entries become property of the sponsor and will not be returned.

Prize Selection/Validations: Winners will be selected in random drawings on or about 7/30/93, by VENTURA ASSOCIATES, INC., an independent judging organization whose decisions are final. Odds of winning are determined by total number of entries received. Circulation of this sweepstakes is estimated not to exceed 200 million. Entrants need not be present to win. All prizes are guaranteed to be awarded and delivered to winners. Winners will be notified by mail and may be required to complete an affidavit of eligibility and release of liability which must be returned within 14 days of date of notification or alternate winners will be selected. Any guest of a trip winner will also be required to execute a release of liability. Any prize notification letter or any prize returned to a participating sponsor, Bantam Doubleday Dell Publishing Group, Inc., its participating divisions or subsidiaries, or VENTURA ASSOCIATES, INC. as undeliverable will be awarded to an alternate winner. Prizes are not transferable. No multiple prize winners except as may be necessary due to unavailability, in which case a prize of equal or greater value will be awarded. Prizes will be awarded approximately 90 days after the drawing. All taxes, automobile license and registration fees, if applicable, are the sole responsibility of the winners. Entry constitutes permission (except where prohibited) to use winners' names and likenesses for publicity purposes without further or other compensation.

Participation: This sweepstakes is open to residents of the United States and Canada, except for the province of Quebec. This sweepstakes is sponsored by Bantam Doubleday Dell Publishing Group, Inc. (BDD), 666 Fifth Avenue, New York, NY 10103. Versions of this sweepstakes with different graphics will be offered in conjunction with various solicitations or promotions by different subsidiaries and divisions of BDD. Employees and their families of BDD, its division, subsidiaries, advertising agencies, and VENTURA ASSOCIATES, INC., are not eligible.

Canadian residents, in order to win, must first correctly answer a time limited arithmetical skill testing question. Void in Quebec and wherever prohibited or restricted by law. Subject to all federal, state, local and provincial laws and regulations.

Prizes: The following values for prizes are determined by the manufacturers' suggested retail prices or by what these items are currently known to be selling for at the time this offer was published. Approximate retail values include handling and delivery of prizes. Estimated maximum retail value of prizes: 1 Grand Prize ($27,500 if merchandise or $25,000 Cash); 1 First Prize ($3,000); 5 Second Prizes ($400 each); 35 Third Prizes ($100 each); 1,000 Fourth Prizes ($9.00 each) ; 1 Early Bird Prize ($5,000); Total approximate maximum retail value is $50,000. Winners will have the option of selecting any prize offered at level won. Automobile winner must have a valid driver's license at the time the car is awarded. Trips are subject to space and departure availability. Certain black-out dates may apply. Travel must be completed within one year from the time the prize is awarded. Minors must be accompanied by an adult. Prizes won by minors will be awarded in the name of parent or legal guardian.

For a list of Major Prize Winners (available after 7/30/93): send a self-addressed, stamped envelope entirely separate from your entry to: Winners Classic Sweepstakes Winners, P.O. Box 825, Gibbstown, NJ 08027. Requests must be received by 6/1/93. DO NOT SEND ANY OTHER CORRESPONDENCE TO THIS P.O. BOX.